# ULTIMATE UNOFFICIAL
# SURVIVAL TACTICS
## FOR
# FORTNITE
## BATTLE ROYALE
## MASTERING GAME SETTINGS FOR VICTORY

# ULTIMATE UNOFFICIAL
# SURVIVAL TACTICS
## FOR
# FORTNITE
## BATTLE ROYALE
## MASTERING GAME SETTINGS FOR VICTORY

## JASON R. RICH

Sky Pony Press
New York

Sky Pony Press books may be purchased in bulk at special discounts for sales promotion, corporate gifts, fund-raising, or educational purposes. Special editions can also be created to specifications. For details, contact the Special Sales Department, Sky Pony Press, 307 West 36th Street, 11th Floor, New York, NY 10018 or info@ skyhorsepublishing.com.

Sky Pony® is a registered trademark of Skyhorse Publishing, Inc.®, a Delaware corporation.

Visit our website at www.skyponypress.com.

10 9 8 7 6 5 4 3 2

Library of Congress Cataloging-in-Publication Data is available on file.

Cover design by Brian Peterson
Cover artwork: iStockphoto

Hardcover ISBN: 978-1-5107-4454-7
E-book ISBN: 978-1-5107-4462-2

Printed in the United States of America

# TABLE OF CONTENTS

# ULTIMATE UNOFFICIAL
# SURVIVAL TACTICS
## FOR
# FORTNITE
## BATTLE ROYALE

# MASTERING GAME SETTINGS FOR VICTORY

# SECTION 1

## OVERVIEW OF *FORTNITE: BATTLE ROYALE*

**A**re you ready to experience an ultra-intense, combat-oriented action/adventure that requires quick thinking and the ability to react faster than your opponents during each firefight? Do you have what it takes to develop and execute perfectly timed, well-planned, creative, and scenario-specific strategies that'll outsmart other gamers in the heat of each battle?

If you answered "yes" to these questions, perhaps you'll now muster up the courage to experience *Fortnite: Battle Royale*—one of the most popular games in the world.

Whether you opt to play this game on a PC, Mac, PlayStation 4, Xbox One, Nintendo Switch, Apple iPhone, Apple iPad, or an Android-based mobile device, prepare yourself to take control of a soldier who gets transported to a mysterious island along with up to 99 other soldiers (each controlled in real time by a different gamer).

Your sole objective is to survive! You want your soldier to be the last person on the island at the end of the match. Everyone else must perish, be defeated, or eliminated in order for you to achieve #1 Victory Royale.

The mysterious island where this adventure takes place is vast and has many unique places to explore. This is what the island map looked like during Season 5. As you'll discover once you begin playing, the island evolves and changes over time, as various game-altering events take place.

While you're trying to outsmart and outfight the enemy soldiers, you'll need to contend with a deadly storm that's continuously expanding and moving, making more and more of the island uninhabitable as each match progresses. The storm-ravaged areas of the island are displayed in pink on the island map.

As you'll discover, to become a truly awesome *Fortnite: Battle Royale* player, you'll need to successfully juggle more than a dozen different tasks. While there are countless strategies you can learn, you'll likely need to spend many hours practicing your exploration, combat, building, and survival skills to ultimately achieve success.

During a firefight, not only do you need to choose the right weapon, based on what's available in your arsenal and the current situation, you'll also need to perfectly aim that weapon and then fire it at the optimal moment to hit your enemy. A headshot will always cause more damage than a body shot, for example. When choosing a weapon, determine if a short-range weapon, mid-range weapon, long-range weapon, explosive weapon, or a projectile explosive weapon (such as a Rocket Launcher) would be best for the job at hand.

*Fortnite: Battle Royale* offers many different weapon options, each of which works slightly differently, and is designed for a specific task (such as close-range, mid-range, or long-range combat). Each type of gun requires compatible ammunition that you'll need to collect and stockpile during each match. Without the right ammunition on hand, a weapon will be useless.

## WHAT YOU'LL LEARN FROM THIS UNOFFICIAL STRATEGY GUIDE

One thing you can do to improve your chances of survival during a match is to fully customize many aspects of your game play experience—ranging from the appearance of your soldier, to the controls you use to perform game-related tasks quickly and efficiently.

How to customize *Fortnite: Battle Royale*'s game-related options and settings, regardless of which gaming system you're using, is the main focus of this unofficial strategy guide.

If you're more interested in actual game play tips and strategies, be sure to pick up a copy of one of the other full-color, unofficial guides by Jason R. Rich. (See page 5.) Visit: www.FortniteGameBooks.com for more information on these and other tip- and strategy-packed guides.

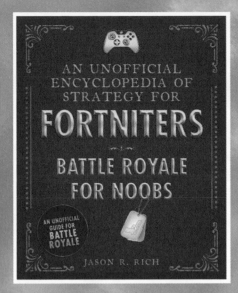

- *An Unofficial Encyclopedia of Strategy for Fortniters: Battle Royale for Noobs*
- *Fortnite Battle Royale Hacks: Surviving the Final Circle*
- *Ultimate Unofficial Survival Tactics for Fortnite Battle Royale: Discover the Island's Best Loot*
- *Ultimate Unofficial Survival Tactics for Fortnite Battle Royale: Sharpshooter Secrets for Mastering Your Arsenal*

## THE GAME'S SOUND EFFECTS ARE EXTREMELY IMPORTANT

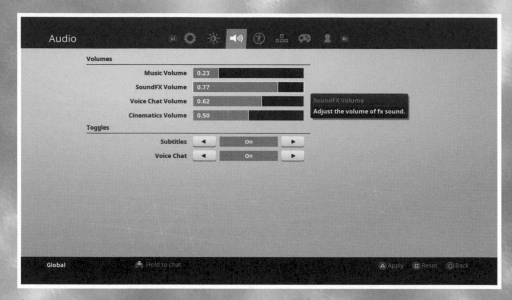

If you're a noob (beginner), there are some settings and options you'll want to customize right away, like options associated with the Audio submenu (shown here). How to access this menu and adjust its settings will be explained shortly.

Sound effects play an essential role in *Fortnite: Battle Royale*. For example, you'll often hear an enemy approaching before he or she can be seen. You'll also hear the sound of chests that are behind walls, floors, or ceilings, even when they're not visible.

Other important sounds to listen for during a match include the roar of an approaching All Terrain Kart's engine, the construction sounds from enemy soldiers who are building, noise created when a soldier uses his or her pickaxe, the opening and closing of doors in a building or structure you're in, and the direction enemy weapon fire is coming from.

To make sure you hear each sound effect the way it was meant to be heard, before a match access the game's Audio submenu. Consider turning down the Music Volume option. Also turn up the SoundFX Volume option.

If you'll be playing the *Fortnite: Battle Royale* Duos or Squads game play mode, for example, and you'll be using an optional gaming headset (with built-in microphone) to speak with your fellow gamers, also turn up the Voice Chat Volume, and be sure the Voice Chat feature is turned on.

Regardless of which gaming system you'll be using to play *Fortnite: Battle Royale*, at the very least, you'll want to connect a pair of good-quality stereo headphones to your gaming system so that you can properly hear the in-game sound effects. Not being able to hear these sound effects will put you at a huge disadvantage.

Anytime you're playing with a partner, squad members, or teammates (in Duos, Squads, or a 50 v 50 game play mode, for example), using a gaming headset with a built-in microphone is an absolute must if you want to be a competitive player.

Many companies, such as Turtle Beach Corp. (www.turtlebeach.com), HyperX (www.hyperxgaming.com), and Razer (www.razer.com), make top-quality wired and wireless (Bluetooth) gaming headsets that work perfectly with all gaming systems.

## DON'T ADJUST GAME SETTINGS RANDOMLY

Before making changes to many of the other game-related settings, first spend time getting acquainted with the game and establishing your own game play style. Then, tweak only those features and functions that'll allow you to improve your performance, speed, accuracy, and success rate. For most noobs, many of the default game-related settings will initially work just fine.

Regardless of your skill level and experience playing *Fortnite: Battle Royale*, don't simply copy the custom settings that top-ranked players use, because each of these players have tweaked the game based on their personal gaming style and the equipment they're using.

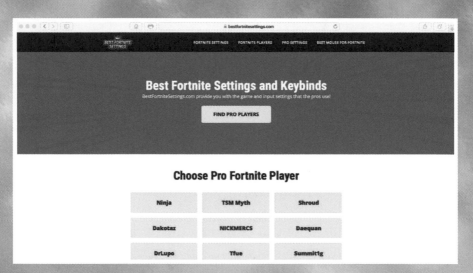

There are many websites, like Best *Fortnite* Settings (www.bestfortnitesettings. com), that reveal the customized settings used by top-ranked players. Use this information as a guideline, but don't just copy another player's settings exactly.

If you copy a top-ranked player's personalized settings, and you're not using the exact same gaming system and equipment as them, your reflexes work at a different speed, or your personal game play style is even a little bit different, that other player's settings won't work well for you. In fact, copying their settings exactly might even make you a worse player.

Which settings to adjust, and how to adjust them, is explained within Sections 2 through 5, based on which gaming system you'll be using.

## HOW TO INSTALL THE GAME AND CREATE AN EPIC GAMES ACCOUNT

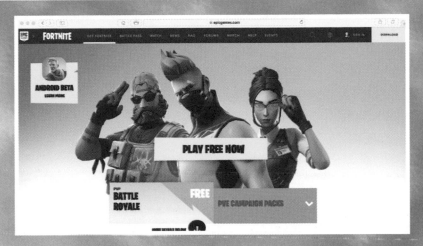

Step one is to download and install *Fortnite: Battle Royale*. Visit **www.Fortnite.com** and click on the Download button that's displayed near the top-right corner of the browser window. PC and Mac gamers can acquire the game directly from the official *Fortnite* website.

After selecting your gaming platform, you'll be redirected to the appropriate place from which you'll be able to download the game— for free. Alternatively use one of these links:

- **Xbox One Users**—Visit the Xbox Marketplace (www. microsoft.com/en-us/p/fortnite-battle-royale/bt5p2x999vh2).
- **PlayStation 4 Users**—Visit the PlayStation Store (https://store.playstation.com/en-gb/product/ EP1464-CUSA07669_00-FORTNITETESTING1).
- **Nintendo Switch Users**—Visit the Nintendo eShop (www. nintendo.com/games/detail/fortnite-switch).
- **Apple iPhone and iPad Users**—Visit the App Store (https://itunes.apple.com/us/app/fortnite/id1261357853).
- **Android Users**—*Fortnite: Battle Royale* is not available from the Google Play Store. Instead, visit http://fortnite.com/android for information about how to download and install the game onto your smartphone or tablet.

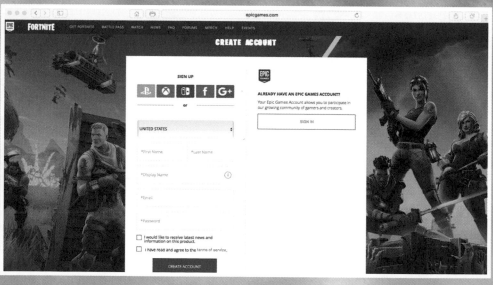

One of your first tasks will be to create a free Epic Games account. You can do this from within the game after it's launched for the first time, or by visiting: www.epic games.com/site/register. During this process, you'll need to create a unique username (between 3 and 16 characters long). This is how you'll be identified in the game when playing with other gamers.

Once your Epic Games account is established, if you'll be playing on a console-based system (a PlayStation 4, Xbox One, or Nintendo Switch), you'll need to link your Epic Games account with your established PlayStation Network, Xbox Live Gold, or My Nintendo account. This only needs to be done once.

If you haven't already done this, access these pages from the Epic Games website to help you:

- **PlayStation 4 Users**—https://epicgames.helpshift.com/a /fortnite/?l=en&s=ps4&f=how-do-i-connect-my-psn-account-to -my-epic-account
- **Xbox One Users**—https://epicgames.helpshift.com/a /fortnite/?s=xbox-one&f=how-do-i-connect-my-xbox-account-to
- -my-epic-account
- **Nintendo Switch Users**—https://epicgames.helpshift .com/a/fortnite/?l=en&s=switch&f=how-do-i-connect-my -nintendo-account-to-my-epic-account

Each time you launch *Fortnite: Battle Royale*, you'll find yourself in the Lobby. It's from here that you can customize a wide range of game-related settings and options prior to participating in a match.

## CUSTOMIZE THE APPEARANCE OF YOUR CHARACTER

One of the customization options available to all gamers, on all gaming platforms, is the ability to choose the appearance of your soldier prior to a match. This is done from the Locker. However, before you can change your soldier's appearance, you'll need to purchase, unlock, or acquire outfits and related items.

Every day within the Item Shop, Epic Games releases a selection of new outfits and items that can be purchased using V-Bucks.

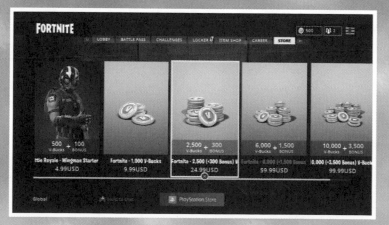

While you can win small bundles of V-Bucks by completing certain tiers, which are part of a Battle Pass, V-Bucks are typically purchased for real money from the Store.

From the Item Shop, you can typically choose from a selection of Featured Items (on the left side of the screen) and Daily Items (on the right side of the screen). These include: outfits with matching back bling (backpack) designs, outfits without a back bling design, separate Glider designs, separate pickaxe designs, and various types of emotes (mostly dance moves).

It's important to understand that any items you purchase, unlock, or acquire are for cosmetic purposes only. They'll make your soldier look lit but give him or her no tactical advantage whatsoever. Despite this, customizing a soldier's appearance is an extremely popular feature.

In addition to purchasing items from the Item Shop, outfits and related items (along with emotes) are offered as prizes for completing challenges associated with a Battle Pass, and sometimes free challenges. To see what prizes are offered for each Battle Pass Tier, from the Lobby access the Battle Pass screen.

A new Battle Pass can be purchased during each gaming season (every two to three months), but this is optional. To learn more about Battle Passes and how they work, visit: www.epicgames.com/fortnite /en-US/battle-pass.

Shown on the previous page is the Sun Strider outfit which was unlocked as a prize after reaching tier 47 in the Season 5 Battle Pass.

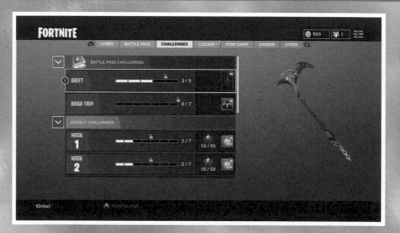

To view the daily free challenges that you can choose to complete in order to unlock prizes (which do not require purchasing a Battle Pass), from the Lobby, access the Challenges screen.

Whether or not you complete each of the tiers in a paid Battle Pass, or attempt to accomplish the free challenges in order to unlock prizes, is entirely up to you.

Some outfits and related items are only available by completing challenges. Others are given away exclusively as part of a Twitch Prime Pack. To acquire a free Twitch Prime Pack, you'll need to have a paid Amazon Prime subscription and a free Twitch.tv account.

For more information about Twitch Prime Packs, visit:

- https://help.twitch.tv/customer/en/portal/articles/2572060 -twitch-prime-guide
- https://epicgames.helpshift.com/a/fortnite/?s=battle-royale&f =twitch-prime-faq

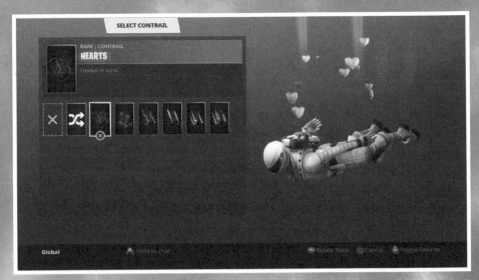

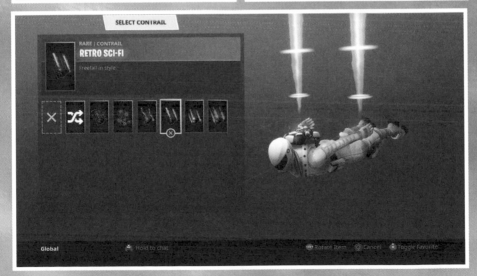

Many types of emotes, as well as contrail designs, can only be acquired by completing challenges or from Twitch Prime Packs, for example. They're not sold within the Item Shop. A contrail is the animation you see as a soldier freefalls after leaping from the Battle Bus.

Most of the soldier customization items are sold from the Item Shop, and the selection changes daily. In fact, since *Fortnite: Battle Royale* was first introduced, hundreds of outfits and thousands of related items have been released. Some outfits, like Leviathan, and its matching items are considered "Legendary." These tend to be more expensive (costing up to 2,000 V-Bucks) but are made available for a very short time. They're limited edition and rare.

Depending on how large of a V-Bucks bundle you purchase, which determines the discount you'll receive, using 2,000 V-Bucks to purchase one outfit, for example, is equivalent to about $20.00 (US).

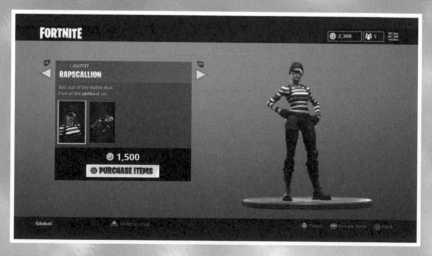

Other outfits and related items are more common and get reintroduced into the Item Shop every few weeks or months. These tend to be less expensive.

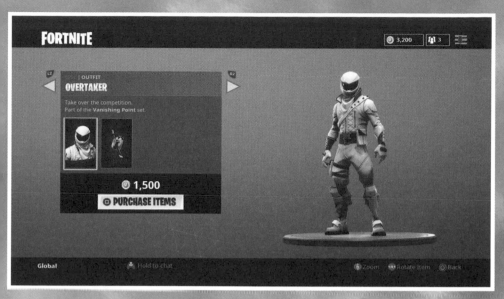

Your soldier's appearance is determined, in part, by the outfit you select. Some outfits, like Overtaker, come bundled with a matching back bling design, although each is considered a separate item within the Locker.

To purchase an outfit that's being showcased within the Item Shop, first buy a bundle of V-Bucks from the Store (using real money), then return to the Item Shop. One at a time, select the item(s) you want to purchase. After purchasing an item and seeing a Successfully Purchased message associated with it (shown here), that item permanently becomes yours, and gets stored within the Locker.

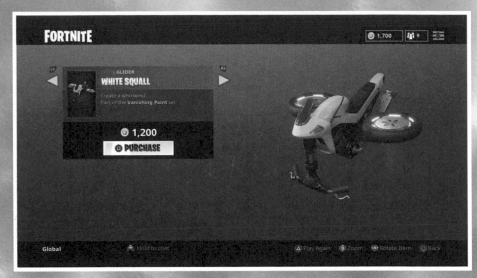

After choosing and purchasing one or more outfits, you have the option to acquire matching pickaxe and Glider designs. Each is sold separately, and all are optional. Once you own a selection of outfits, back bling designs, pickaxe designs, and Glider designs, you can mix and match them however you want from the Locker to create a unique look for your soldier.

From the Item Shop, a selection of emotes (mostly dance moves) are also offered daily. During each match, you can load six different emotes into your soldier's Emotes Menu and use them during a match to express emotion or personality.

Some gamers use a dance move as a greeting. Others use them to gloat after defeating an enemy. Some gamers make their soldiers break out into dance just for fun, at random times during a match when it's safe. The many different dance moves available from the Item Shop are each sold separately, and also get stored within the Locker once they've been acquired.

Before a match, from the Lobby, access the Locker to customize your soldier. On the left side of the Locker screen, under the Account and Equipment heading, there are seven slots—each allows you to customize something related to your soldier (or are game related). Shown here on the extreme left, choose the Banner option to customize a personal banner. After selecting this option, you can custom-design your own personal banner. Anyone can do this for free.

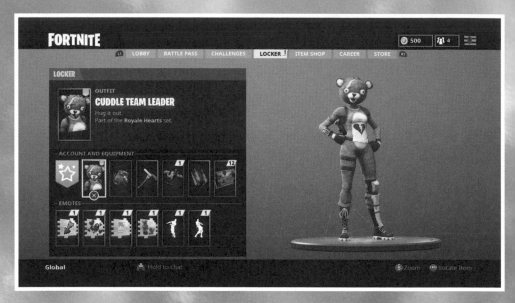

Highlight and select the Outfit slot to choose from the outfits that are stored within the Locker (and that have already been purchased, unlocked, or acquired).

On the left side of the screen are the available outfit options. On the right side of the screen is what your soldier looks like in the selected outfit. A growing number of outfits have several styles you can also unlock and choose from. If this is available for the chosen outfit, select the Edit Style option that's display near the top-left corner of the screen.

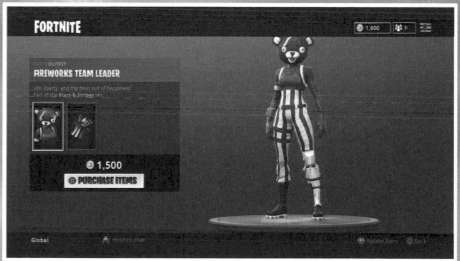

Some Legendary outfits, like Omen and Raven, can make your soldier look tough or mysterious. Others, like Magnus and Fireworks Team Leader, have some type of theme (related to something happening as part of the game's ongoing storyline, or an event/holiday happening in the real world, like July 4th or Christmas).

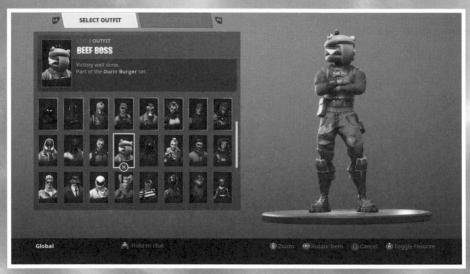

Others, including Beef Boss, Zoey, Rex, and Chomp Sr., are more lighthearted or ridiculous. Once you've selected an outfit for your soldier to wear during a match, all of the other gamers you encounter during the match will see it.

After choosing an outfit, return to the Locker. Next, select and highlight the Back Bling option, followed by the Pickaxe option, Glider option, and Contrail option. Just like when you choose an outfit, the available designs are displayed on the left side of the screen, and the currently selected design is displayed on the right side of the screen.

You're also able to choose a Loading Screen graphic that only you will see each time *Fortnite: Battle Royale* loads.

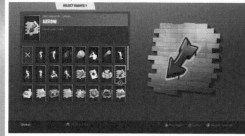

From below the Emotes heading on the main Locker screen, one at a time, select one of the six Emotes slots. Here, the one in the bottom-left corner of the screen is selected.

Choose one of the available emotes that you want to make available during the upcoming match. The Select Emote screen shows all of the unlocked graphic icon emotes, as well as the dance moves and spray paint tags that are available to you. One at a time, select one emote for each of the six slots.

When you highlight a dance move on the left side of the screen within the Locker, you'll see your soldier demonstrate that move on the right side of the screen.

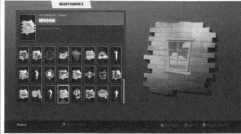

Likewise, when you select a spray paint tag on the left side of the screen, you'll see what it looks like on the right side of the screen within the Locker.

After choosing your emotes, anytime you're in the pre-deployment area or during a match, to use an emote, access this Emotes Menu, and one at a time, select the emote you want to show off.

You can use two or three different spray paint tags at the same location to create some eye-catching graffiti on the island, or mix a few dance moves together to show off some lit choreography.

When you're done customizing the appearance of your soldier from the Locker, return to the Lobby. From here, you can either choose a game play mode and then enter into a match and begin playing *Fortnite: Battle Royale*, or you can access the game's menu, and then access a variety of settings-related submenus, to personalize your game play experience and tweak how you'll interact with the game.

Anytime Epic Games has an important announcement related to *Fortnite: Battle Royale*, you'll see it displayed in the bottom-center of the Lobby screen.

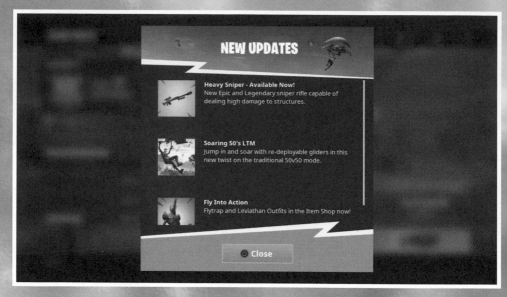

Meanwhile, anytime something new is added to the game, a New Updates pop-up window, like this one (or a News screen), will appear when you launch the game.

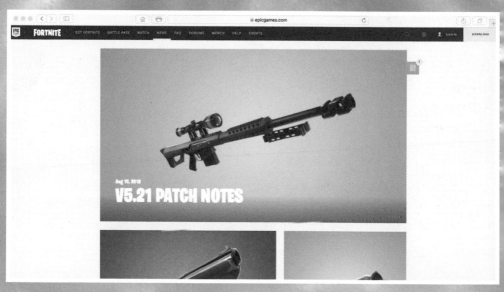

You can also visit: www.epicgames.com/fortnite/en-US/news to read about the latest updates and changes made to the game. These website updates are called "Patch Notes."

# HOW TO TWEAK THE GAME'S SETTINGS

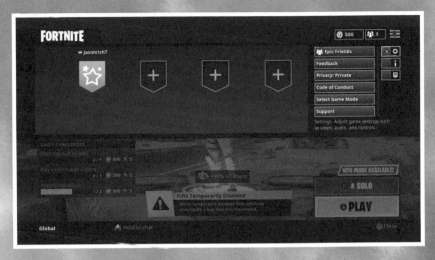

Regardless of which gaming system you're using, to adjust the settings, you'll need to access the game's main menu from the Lobby. To do this, press the Menu button on your controller (or keyboard/mouse). From this menu (displayed in the top-right corner of the screen), highlight and select the gear-shaped Settings icon to access the Settings submenus.

# THE GAME MENU

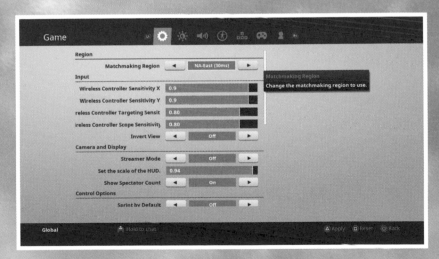

The options available from the Settings menu are divided into a group of submenus. Access one of these at a time by scrolling through the menu icons displayed along the top-center of the screen, starting with the Display and Game submenus. The Game menu offers a large selection of customizable options, some related to the sensitivity of the controller (or mouse). It's shown here on a PS4.

The entire focus of Section 2—Discover What You Can Do from the Game Submenu is on what options are included within the Game submenu and how to take advantage of them.

## DISPLAY

The Display submenu applies to the PC, Mac, and mobile versions of the game—not the console-based versions. You'll find more information about how and why you might want to adjust these options within Section 3—Customizing Your Game Play Experience on a PC or Mac, as well as Section 5—Personalizing Your *Fortnite: Battle Royale* Experience on a Mobile Device.

PC and Mac gamers should also check out Section 3—Customizing Your Game Play Experience on a PC or Mac for more information about customizing the game. See Section 4—Tweaking the Game Settings on a Console-Based System if you're using a console-based system (PS4, Xbox One, or Nintendo Switch). Mobile device users should see Section 5—Personalizing Your *Fortnite: Battle Royale* Experience on a Mobile Device for details about how to customize *Fortnite: Battle Royale* when playing on an iOS or Android smartphone or tablet.

# BRIGHTNESS CALIBRATION

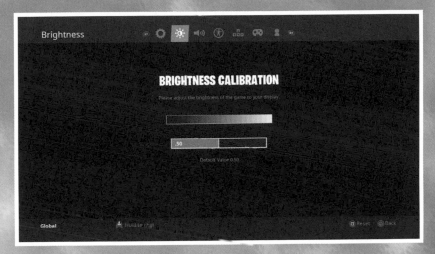

Use this slider to adjust the brightness of your game screen. Typically, the default setting (around .50) is fine. However, if you're playing in a room that's very bright or very dark, you may want to adjust this slider so you can see more vivid colors and detail within the game while looking at your TV screen or monitor.

# AUDIO

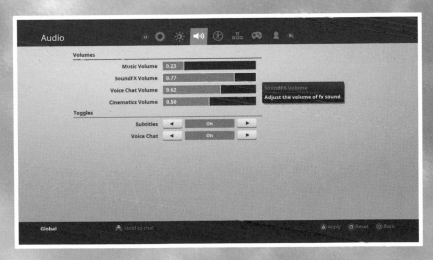

From this menu, adjust the Music Volume, SoundFX Volume, Voice Chat Volume, and Cinematics Volume separately. When playing *Fortnite: Battle Royale* (as opposed to *Fortnite: Save the World*), the Cinematics Volume isn't too important, so you can ignore it.

So that you're able to hear the sound effects within the game, consider turning down the Music Volume and turning up the SoundFX Volume. Unless you'll be playing Duos, Squads, or other game play modes that require you to talk with your partner, squad mates, or team members, you can turn down Voice Chat Volume, or turn off the Voice Chat feature altogether.

## ACCESSIBILITY

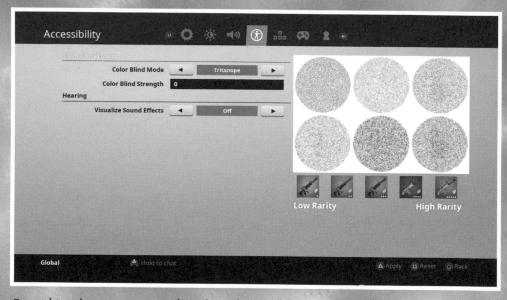

From this submenu screen, adjust the colors the game will display if you're color blind. If you have a hearing impairment, you're also able to turn on the Visualize Sound Effects option, so you can see graphics and icons on the screen that replicate the sound effects you'd otherwise hear (like footsteps, doors opening and closing, gunfire, etc.).

# INPUT

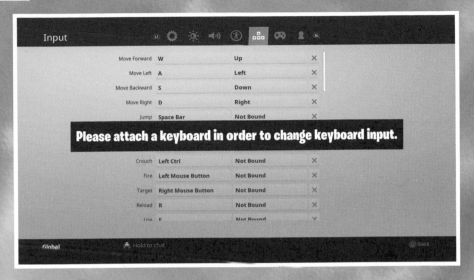

This menu is specifically for gamers using a keyboard and mouse to control their gaming experience, so it mostly applies to PC and Mac users, although it is possible to connect an optional keyboard and mouse to your console-based gaming system. Section 3 focuses on the options and settings offered by this submenu. When no keyboard or mouse is connected to a console (in this case a PS4), a message that says "Please attach a keyboard in order to change keyboard input" appears on the screen.

Here, the same submenu was accessed from the PC version of *Fortnite: Battle Royale*, and all of the submenu options are displayed.

# WIRELESS CONTROLLER

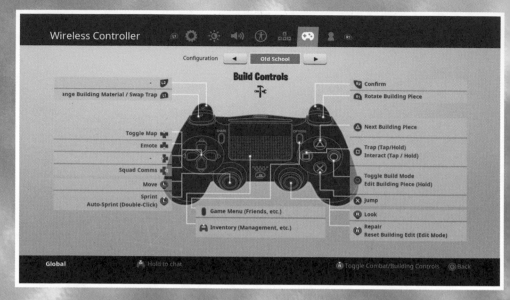

This menu mainly applies to console-based gamers. Built into *Fortnite: Battle Royale* are four controller layouts—Old School, Quick Builder, Combat Pro, and Builder Pro. See Section 4 for tips on choosing which is the best for you, based on your personal gaming style.

It is also possible, however, to link a wireless controller with a PC or Mac. For console gamers, playing *Fortnite: Battle Royale* with a top-quality wireless controller will help improve the speed that you can do things within the game. If you're a Nintendo Switch user, for example, consider linking an optional Nintendo Switch Pro Controller ($69.99 US) or a similar controller to your gaming system.

Beginning at the start of Season 6, Epic Games introduced a button binding feature to the Wireless Controller menu. When you choose the Custom option, you can assign specific in-game actions and tasks to specific controller buttons, based on your personal game play style.

# ACCOUNT

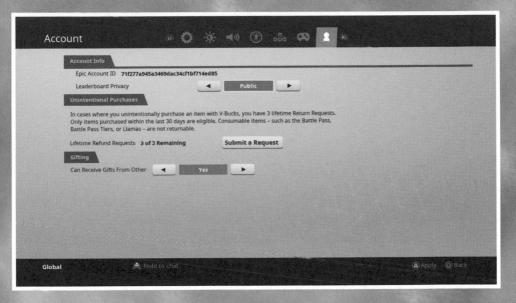

To manage your Epic Games account, access the Account submenu (shown here). You can also manage your account online by visiting: https://accounts.epicgames. com/register. If you already have an Epic Games account, click on the Sign In option displayed at the bottom of the screen. Then, if you've forgotten your password, click on the Forgot Your Password? option.

## JUMP INTO YOUR FIRST *FORTNITE: BATTLE ROYALE* MATCH

To play *Fortnite: Battle Royale*, your gaming system must have a high-speed and continuous Internet connection.

When your gaming system connects to Epic Games' game servers via the Internet, it'll automatically choose a server in your geographic region that offers the fastest connection. You can manually change the server you connect to, but this could slow down your connection speed with Epic Games' servers.

The Matchmaking Region (server) options include: Auto (the default option), North America—East Coast, North America—West Coast, Europe, Oceania, Brazil, and Asia.

Having the fastest possible Internet connection works to your advantage. If the connection is too slow, the game will glitch and you could wind up losing a battle and getting defeated because the game didn't react quickly enough.

For this reason, anytime you're playing *Fortnite: Battle Royale* from a mobile device, for example, consider using a Wi-Fi Internet connection as opposed to an often slower 4G/LTE connection.

# CHOOSE YOUR DESIRED GAME PLAY MODE

When you're ready to start playing *Fortnite: Battle Royale*, return to the Lobby and then access the Choose Game Mode option. There are three permanent game play modes—Solo, Duos, and Squads.

- **Solo**—Choose this game play mode to experience *Fortnite: Battle Royale* on your own. It'll be you against up to 99 other gamers, each controlling their own soldier in real time.
- **Duos**—Team up with one other player (either an online friend or a random gamer) and experience a match together. Throughout the match, communicate in real time (if you're both using a gaming headset), so you can plan and execute perfectly timed and well-coordinated attacks on your enemies. You're also able to revive your partner if he or she gets injured, plus share weapons, ammo, loot items, and resources.
- **Squads**—This game play mode allows you to team up with three other gamers (either online friends or random gamers) and work together as a four-soldier squad to defeat the up to twenty-four other four-person squads participating in the match. In this game play mode, constantly communicating with your squad mates and working together will be your key to achieving #1 Victory Royale.

Each week Epic Games introduces at least one or two (sometimes three) temporary game play modes that offer a totally different gaming experience. For example, when Playground mode is offered, this gives you 55 minutes to:

- Explore the island
- Experiment using various weapons and loot items
- Practice building
- Participate in mock battles
- Practice driving an All Terrain Kart
- Take advantage of special features added to the specific version of the Playground mode that's being offered.

## CHOOSE TO PLAY WITH ONLINE FRIENDS OR RANDOM GAMERS

Anytime you choose to play a Duos or Squads game or select any game play mode that allows you to work with other gamers, from the Choose Game Mode screen you must select whether you want to play with online friends or random gamers.

Displayed just above the Accept button is the Fill (shown on the left) / Don't Fill (shown on the right) option. If you want to play with random gamers, select the Fill option after choosing an appropriate game play mode. However, if you want to manually invite one or more of your online friends (or accept an invitation from an online friend) select the Don't Fill option and return to the Lobby.

Before selecting the Play option, either respond to one of the yellow invitation banners displayed near the center of the screen (which appear to the right or left of your soldier) or highlight and select one of the "+" icons for each player you want to send an invitation to. Next, access the Party Finder menu. (Shown here on an iPad Pro.)

From the Party Finder menu, highlight and select one online friend at a time and select the Invite option to invite that person to a Duos or Squads match, for example, or choose the Join option to accept an invitation and join a party (which is a group of gamers who want to play *Fortnite: Battle Royale* together as a squad or team, depending on which game play mode is selected).

When you're ready to begin a match, from the Lobby, select the Play option. You'll be transported to the pre-deployment area, where you'll wait for up to 99 other gamers to join the match.

Once everyone joins the game, all players climb aboard the Battle Bus and get transferred to the island, where your adventure awaits.

# CUSTOMIZE YOUR BACKPACK INVENTORY

At any time during a match, access the Backpack Inventory screen to see the collection of weapons, ammo, loot items, and resources your soldier is currently carrying within their backpack. Here you can see details related to a "Rare" (blue) Bolt-Action Sniper Rifle. Displayed in the top-left corner of the screen is information about the weapon's DPS (Damage Per Second) Rating, Damage Rating, Fire Rate, Magazine Size, and Reload Time.

From the Backpack Inventory screen, you can handle several tasks, including:

Learn about a specific type of weapon or loot item your soldier is carrying by highlighting and selecting it. Shown here, a Slurp Juice loot item has been selected. Based on information displayed in the top-left corner of the screen, you can see that this soldier has two of this item, and that when it's consumed, it'll replenish a soldier's Health and Shields meters up to 75 HP points over time (37.5 seconds to be exact).

Learn about specific types of ammo, how much you have on hand, and the types of weapons each of the five different types of ammo works with. Again, look to the top-left corner of the Backpack Inventory screen. This time you'll see that Ammo: Heavy Bullets is selected. This type of ammunition is used with high-caliber weapons, including sniper rifles. Currently, this soldier is holding 78 rounds of Heavy Bullets ammunition.

When playing a game play mode that involves a partner, squad mates, or team members, you can share any of what you're carrying. To do this, stand close to the soldier you want to share with, access the Backpack Inventory screen, highlight and select a weapon, ammo type, loot item, or resource type (stone is selected here), and select the Drop option.

If you're holding multiples of the selected item, such as 693 stone (shown here), choose to share only some of what you're carrying. After selecting the Drop option, use this slider to choose how much of the selected ammo, loot item, or resource you want to share. In this case, 346 stone out of 693 is selected. Choose the Drop option. That item will be dropped, and the soldier you want to share with can then pick it up.

You can drop anything from your backpack at any time in order to free up space. However, if a partner, squad mate, or team member is not around to pick it up, what you drop will be left on the ground. Any other soldier (including your enemies) can then grab it.

Keep in mind, a soldier can carry a maximum of 1,000 wood, 1,000 stone, and 1,000 metal in their backpack simultaneously.

Continuously displayed on the main game screen are the up to five items (excluding the pickaxe) that your soldier is carrying. To speed up the time it takes you to access the more commonly used weapons or items, you're able to rearrange your backpack. To do this, access the Backpack Inventory screen. Highlight and select one item (the Shield Potion is shown here), and then use the directional arrows to move it to a different slot within your backpack.

On the right, the Shield Potion is positioned within the left-most backpack inventory slot. On the left, the same item has been moved to the right-most position within your backpack. You can see this in the lower-right corner of the screen.

Some weapons in *Fortnite: Battle Royale*, like the Bolt-Action Sniper Rifle, have a very slow reload time. One way to avoid the wait while a weapon reloads in between shots is to grab two similar or identical weapons. After each shot, instead of waiting for the reload, place the similar or identical weapon in the backpack slot directly next to the first weapon, and quickly switch between them. This way, you can keep shooting with a much shorter delay.

Customizing which backpack slot you store a weapon and loot item in is one way you can speed up the process of switching between them. During an intense battle, even a fraction of a second can make a huge difference when it comes to missing a shot versus making a direct hit and defeating your enemy.

Get into the habit of storing particular types of weapons and loot items within specific slots, so you automatically know where each is and don't have to think too much about it as you go from match to match. For example, always place your most essential weapons in the left-most slots, and your loot items in the right-most slots.

# SECTION 2

## DISCOVER WHAT YOU CAN DO FROM THE GAME SUBMENU

Regardless of which gaming system you're using to play *Fortnite: Battle Royal*, each offers a similar Game submenu, which is accessible by accessing the game's main menu, and then selecting the gear-shaped Settings icon.

## THE GAME SUBMENU'S OPTIONS

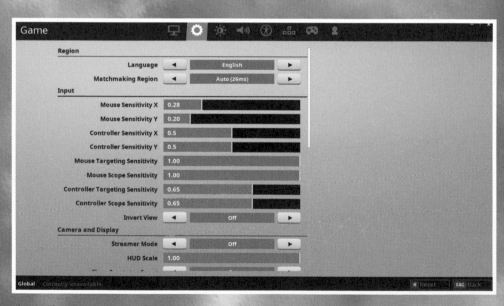

This is the top portion of the Game submenu of *Fortnite: Battle Royale* running on a PC. To see all of the options offered by this menu, you'll need to scroll down. This menu is almost identical on the console-based versions and mobile versions.

This menu is divided into sections labeled Region, Input, Camera and Display, Control Options, and Feedback. The following sections explain each option available.

Once you make changes to any of the options offered by this menu, be sure to press the appropriate controller (keyboard) button for the **Apply** command to save your changes. Your customizations will remain active until you return to this menu and make additional changes.

Use the **Reset** command to return all of the options offered by this submenu to their default settings. Use the **Back** command to exit out of the menu *without* saving your changes. The Apply, Reset, and Back commands can be found in the bottom-right corner of the menu screen.

At the top-center of this screen on some gaming systems are two tabs labeled Game and HUD. We'll start by explaining the options offered by selecting the Game tab. Keep in mind, not all of these options are offered on all gaming systems.

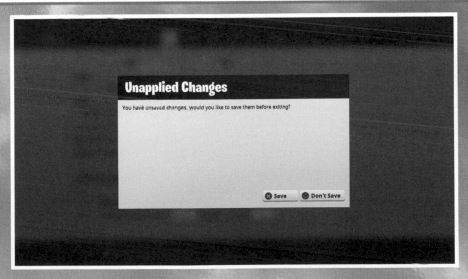

If you've made changes to any options within the Game menu, but then use the Back command, this pop-up window will appear asking if you want to Save or Don't Save Your Unapplied Changes before exiting the menu and returning to the Lobby. (Shown here on a PS4.)

## REGION

**Language**—Choose the language you want text within the game to be displayed in. This option is available in the PC and Mac versions of the game, but not all other versions.

**Matchmaking Region**—The default setting for this option is Auto. When Auto is selected, your gaming system will connect to the closest Epic Games server, based on the fastest connection speed that can be established. In parentheses, you'll see the connection speed in milliseconds. The goal is to achieve the fastest connection speed possible to avoid glitches and lagging when actually playing the game.

Instead of choosing the Auto option, you can manually select between North America—East Coast, North America—West Coast, Europe, Oceania, Brazil, or Asia; however, the farther away you get from your home region, the slower the Internet connection will likely be. If you're from the East Coast of the United States, for example, and choose the Europe server, your connection will be slower, but when the game matches you up with other players for each of your matches, those gamers will be from European countries.

## INPUT / CONTROL OPTIONS

The majority of the options offered under this heading have a slider associated with them. This allows you to precisely fine-tune the setting to fit your personal gaming style, as well as the equipment you're using.

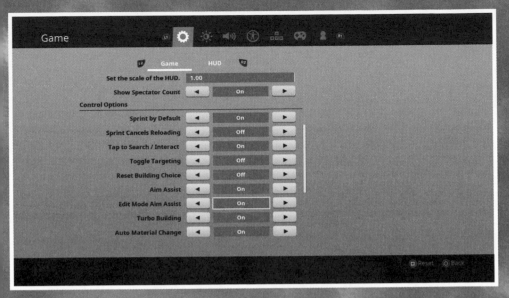

You'll need to scroll down on the Game menu to see more of the available options. (Shown here on a PS4.)

Anytime you're adjusting an option that offers a slider, as opposed to an on/off switch, make small and subtle changes. For example, if the default setting is 0.5, don't change it to 1.0 all at once. Boost it up to 0.6 or 0.7, play a few matches, see if you like the change, and then decide whether to increase or decrease the setting based on how your controller or mouse responds.

**Control (Mouse) Sensitivity X—**Using a slider, this option allows you to adjust the sensitivity of your wireless controller or mouse for the X axis (horizontal movement). The default setting is 0.5, but many gamers prefer this control to be more sensitive and adjust it to between 0.7 and 0.9. By doing this, you'll be able to move your soldier faster and with less effort.

**Control (Mouse) Sensitivity Y—**Using a slider, this option allows you to adjust the sensitivity of your wireless controller or mouse for the Y axis (vertical movement). The default setting is 0.5, but many gamers prefer this control to be more sensitive and adjust it to between 0.7 and 0.9. By doing this, you'll be able to move your soldier faster and with less effort.

Whatever you adjust the Control (Mouse) Sensitivity X setting to should be the same as what you set the Control (Mouse) Sensitivity Y setting to, but this too is a matter of personal preference.

**Controller (Mouse) Targeting Sensitivity**—After pressing the Aim button to target a weapon, this option controls how sensitive the targeting controls are to your movements. The default option is 0.65, but some gamers prefer to make this option more sensitive and boost it to between 0.7 and 0.9. This is a matter of personal preference.

**Controller (Mouse) Scope Sensitivity**—Anytime you're using a rifle with a scope and you press the Aim button, a zoomed-in scope view is displayed, allowing you to much more precisely target your enemy. The scope targeting will be more sensitive if you boost this slider from its 0.65 default setting to between 0.7 and 0.9. Again, you'll want to experiment to determine a setting that works with your personal gaming style and equipment.

**Invert View (On/Off)**—This option reverses the controls for having your soldier look up and down within a match. When turned off, if you point the Look directional controller or mouse option up, your soldier will look up. If you point the Look directional controller or mouse option down, your soldier will look down. However, when you turn on this option, these settings are reversed. Pressing the Look directional controller or mouse option down will cause your soldier to look up and pressing the Look directional controller or mouse option up will cause your soldier to look down.

**Motion Enable (On/Off)**—This option is not available on all gaming systems. It works on the Nintendo Switch and mobile versions, for example. When turned on, when you're holding the gaming system and move it around, this will impact the movement of your view. It doesn't offer gamers a competitive advantage, but it does allow you to see things from a different perspective simply by moving around the gaming system as opposed to moving the Look directional controller (which continues to function in the same way it normally does).

**Motion Sensitivity Not Targeting**—Use this option to adjust the sensitivity of the controls used to move your soldier around while he or she is not targeting a weapon. In other words, when the soldier is walking, running, jumping, or tiptoeing around the island. The more you boost this slider to the right, the more sensitive the controls will be. This option is not available on all gaming systems.

**Motion Sensitivity Targeting**—This option controls the sensitivity of your soldier's motion controls once the Aim button has been pressed and they're targeting a weapon (with the exception of a scoped rifle). When you boost this slider, which is not available on all gaming systems, the target icon will be more sensitive and move with even the slightest touch. With practice, this option can help you improve your aim. Be careful not to make this function too sensitive or aiming accurately will become even more challenging.

**Motion Sensitivity Scoped**—This feature, which is not available on all gaming systems, works just like the Motion Sensitivity Targeting option, but is only active when you're using a rifle with a scope and you zoom in and use the scope view to target your enemies.

**Motion Sensitivity Harvesting Tool**—Also not available on all gaming systems, this option allows you to control how sensitive the controls will be when using your soldier's pickaxe. The more you move this slider to the right, the more sensitive the pickaxe will be to movement controls.

## CAMERA AND DISPLAY

**Streamer Mode**—If you plan to live stream your game play on the Internet, one thing that could put you at a huge disadvantage is if the people watching your stream wind up in the same match as you. By watching your stream, they can see information on your screen that as an enemy, they would not normally be able to see. By turning on this feature, less information is displayed on the screen that would help someone watching your live stream simultaneously defeat your soldier during a match.

**Set the Scale of the HUD**—HUD stands for "Heads Up Display." By default, this slider (which is not available on all gaming systems) is set at 1.0 (or 100 percent). When you decrease this setting, the information displayed on the main game screen pertaining to your soldier's inventory, collected resources, and the Location Map, for example, are shrunk down and take up less space on the screen. This potentially makes them harder to read but frees up more space on the screen for you to see the action.

On the left, this shows the scale of the HUD at 1.0 (100 percent) on a PS4.

On the right, the same information is displayed, but the scale of the HUD is at 0.40. Notice how much smaller various icons appear on the screen, particularly in the bottom-right, top-right, and top-left corners.

**HUD Scale**—Instead of controlling the size of all on-screen icons at once, the mobile edition of *Fortnite: Battle Royale* allows you to customize the size of each icon individually. How to do this is explained within Section 5.

**Show Spectator Count (On/Off)**—Once gamers are eliminated from a match, they automatically enter Spectator mode, which allows them to watch the remainder of a match from another player's perspective. If you're playing a Duos match and your partner outlives you, you'll be able to watch the game from their perspective. When playing a Squads game, Spectator mode allows you to watch the game from the perspective of a former squad mate. In Solo mode, you'll start off in Spectator mode seeing the perspective of the soldier who eliminated you from the match. When turned on, this feature allows you to see how many gamers are currently watching you play.

**Peripheral Lighting (On/Off)**—On some gaming systems, you can turn this feature on in order to display more detailed lighting effects during the game.

## CONTROL OPTIONS

**Sprint by Default (On/Off)**—By default, when you make your soldier move forward, he or she will walk, unless you hold down the Run button or Crouch button (to tiptoe). When turned on, the default will be for your soldier to run. If you then press the Run button on the controller or keyboard, they'll walk.

**Sprint Cancels Reloading (On/Off)**—When turned on, your soldier's weapon can reload at the same time you're running.

**Tap to Search / Interact (On/Off)**—Anytime you approach a chest, Ammo Box, or Loot Llama, by default it's necessary to press and hold down the Search button to open it. When this feature is turned on, you simply need to tap the Search button instead of holding it down. Turning on this feature could save you a small amount of time when opening a chest, Ammo Box, or Loot Llama.

**Toggle Targeting (On/Off)**—Anytime you're using a ranged weapon and press the Aim button, aiming mode will remain on until you tap the Aim button again to revert to the normal view. When this feature is turned on, you'll need to press and hold the Aim button when aiming a weapon. When aiming a weapon, your soldier moves slower if you attempt to make him or her walk, run, or tiptoe.

**Reset Building Choice (On/Off)**—When you enter into Building mode and select a building tile (such as a wall, floor/ceiling, ramp/ stairs, or pyramid-shaped tile), the game will remember your last selection used, and return you to that building tile shape the next time you enter into Building mode. When you turn this feature on, your building tile choice will reset each time you enter into Building mode.

**Aim Assist (On/Off)**—Turning on this option will make it a bit easier to accurately aim your weapons. As you become really skilled at playing *Fortnite: Battle Royale*, you might want to turn off this feature to give yourself more of a challenge. However, noobs should definitely turn on this option.

**Edit Mode Aim Assist (On/Off)**—When in Building mode and using the Edit feature to add windows, doors, or other holes to a tile, this option makes it slightly easier and faster to select tiles to edit. In other words, if used correctly, turning on this feature could help you speed up your overall building speed—but whether you turn it on or off, perfecting your building skills will require a lot of practice.

**Turbo Building (On/Off)**—While you're in Building mode, by turning on this feature, you're able to select a building tile and building material, and then keep building with that tile until you run out of resources, simply by holding down the build button. Turning on this feature makes building faster and easier, especially when it comes to building ramps or bridges.

**Auto Material Change (On/Off)**—Based on the resources you've collected, your soldier is able to build using wood, stone, or metal. When this feature is turned off, if you run out of one resource, you'll manually need to switch to an alternative resource to keep building. By turning on this feature, however, the game will automatically switch resources for you once you run out of the one you're using. This way, you can keep building until you're totally out of all resources. This feature can increase your building speed when turned on.

**Controller Auto-Run (On/Off)**—By turning on this feature, instead of pressing and holding down the Run button to make your soldier run, you can quickly double-click the Run button and your soldier will keep running until you press the Run button again to revert back to walking (or standing still). When you need to run a long distance to escape the storm, turning on Auto-Run allows you to rest your fingers and not have to hold down a controller button. Consider turning on this option.

**Auto Open Doors (On/Off)**—Anytime your soldier approaches a door, either in a pre-built structure or a structure that they've built and added a door to, it's typically necessary to press the Open button on the controller or keyboard to manually open the door and then proceed inside. When this feature is turned on, a door will automatically open as your soldier approaches it. If you want to close the door behind your soldier after they enter, you'll still need to manually press the door open/close button.

**Auto Pickup Weapons (On/Off)**—Your soldier's backpack has five slots in which you can grab and store up to five different weapons or loot items. When this feature is turned on, anytime you approach a weapon that's lying on the ground, if there's an open slot within your soldier's backpack, he or she will automatically pick it up. However, if the backpack is full, you'll still need to manually pick up a weapon, which will replace the weapon or item your soldier is currently holding.

# FEEDBACK

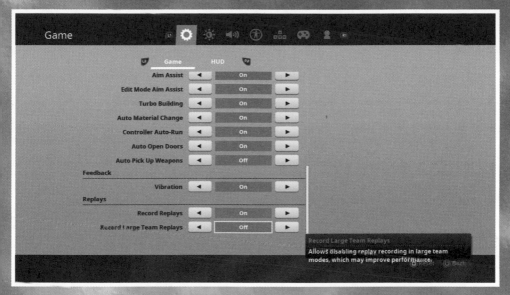

You'll need to scroll down on the Game menu to see more of the available options. (Shown here on a PS4.)

**Rumble/Vibration (On/Off)**—Console gamers that are using a wireless controller that has a rumble or vibration feature can turn on or off this feature when playing *Fortnite: Battle Royale*. When turned on, your controller will vibrate (rumble) when you're hit by a weapon, shooting a weapon, or get caught in an explosion, for example.

**Power Saving Mode (On/Off)**—This feature is offered on gaming systems, including the Nintendo Switch, laptop computers (PC or Mac), and mobile devices that can use battery power to operate. When turned on, the game will use less battery power by scaling down its power consumption while you're playing. Certain less-essential gaming features will be shut down as needed.

## REPLAYS

**Record Replays**—Anytime you're playing *Fortnite: Battle Royale*, the game can automatically record each match, so you can watch, edit, and share a replay. The video file gets stored within your gaming system's internal storage (or on an optional memory card). Saving replays requires a lot of storage space, so only turn on this option if you know you'll want to play back, edit, and potentially share your matches.

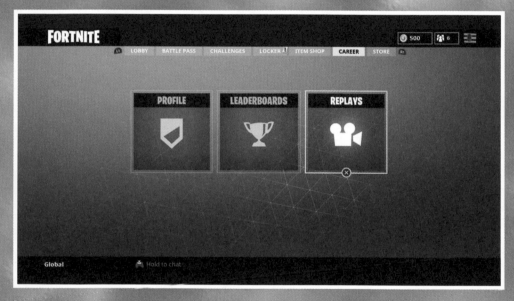

Once you've recorded a match, replay it using on-screen controls to play, pause, re-wind, or fast-forward through the action. To do this, from the Lobby access the Career screen (shown here), and select the Replays option. Choose which replay you want to watch from the listing that's displayed.

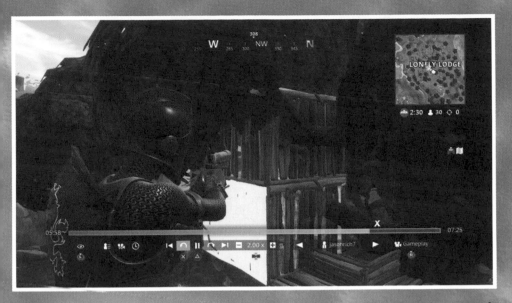

Use the controls displayed along the bottom of the screen to manage a wide range of playback features, such as the playback speed and the viewing perspective.

You're able to watch the match from your own soldier's perspective, through the eyes of another soldier, or from a flying drone's point of view. For additional tips on using the game's playback system, visit: www.epicgames.com/fortnite/en-US/news/fortnite -battle-royale-replay-system or www.vg247.com/2018/05/15/fortnite-replay-system -guide-tips.

**Record Large Team Replays**—If offered by your gaming system, this feature will record Squads and 50 v 50 matches, for example, that require an even greater amount of storage space to save, due to the large file size created.

## HUD OPTIONS

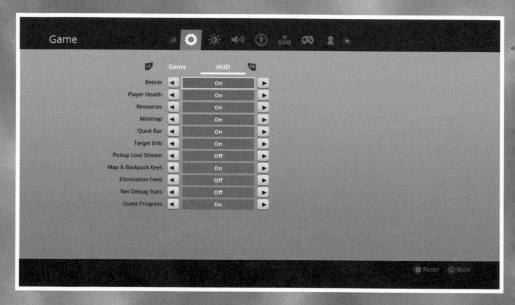

On most gaming systems, once you select the Game submenu, near the top-center of the screen you'll see two tabs. They're labeled Game and HUD. Select the HUD option to determine what information you want displayed on the game screen. If you want to remove clutter from the screen so you can focus more on the action, turn off the features you don't deem important.

By toggling the on/off switch, determine which of the following pieces of information you want displayed on the screen. If you want to see the information, turn the feature on.

- Reticle (targeting crosshairs)—Should be left on.
- Player Health—Should be left on.
- Resources—Should be left on.
- Minimap (Location Map)—Should be left on.

- Quick Bar—Should be left on.
- Target Info—Should be left on.
- Pickup Loot Stream—You can turn this on or off, based on personal preference.
- Map & Backpack Keys—Should be left on.
- Net Debug Stats—Should be turned off to remove on-screen clutter.
- Quest Progress—Should be turned off when playing *Fortnite: Battle Royale* but turned on if you're playing the *Fortnite: Save the World* game.
- Elimination Feed—This is a real-time message that pops up on the screen each time a solider is eliminated from the match. The feed message says who eliminated the soldier and how they were eliminated.

# SECTION 3

## CUSTOMIZING YOUR GAME PLAY EXPERIENCE ON A PC OR MAC

From the Settings menu, the Display submenu offers a wide range of options that can be fine-tuned based on your computer's hardware. Then, you can totally customize how you'll interact with the game by accessing the Input menu and assigning individual keys and mouse buttons with specific game features and functions.

To enhance your gaming experience, many computer users opt to connect a specialized gaming keyboard, gaming mouse, gaming headset, or controller to their computer to increase the response time of their actions and improve their overall speed, especially when participating in battles or building.

To access the Display and Input submenus, from the Lobby, click on the Menu icon that's displayed in the top-right corner of the screen. It looks like three horizontal lines.

From the menu, click on the gear-shaped Settings icon that's displayed near the top-right corner of the screen.

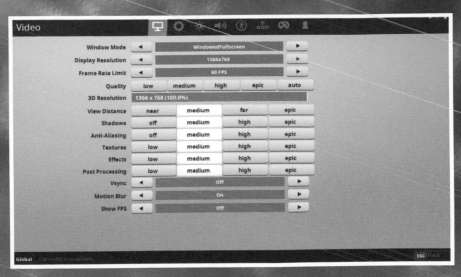

Along the top-center of the screen are the icons for the various settings-related submenus. On the extreme left is the Display menu (shown here).

When viewing the Video (Display) menu, make any changes using your mouse. As soon as you change anything, the Apply button will appear in the bottom-right corner of the screen. To save your changes, be sure to click on the Apply button before exiting from this submenu. If you want to exit without making any changes, press the ESC key on the keyboard.

## ADJUSTING THE VIDEO (DISPLAY) SUBMENU OPTIONS

On a PC or Mac, the Video (Display) submenu offers the following options:

**Window Mode—**There are three options for this setting, including: Windowed, Full Screen, and Windowed Full Screen. Select Windowed to play *Fortnite: Battle Royale* within a window. This makes it quick and easy to switch between applications. Use the Full Screen option to showcase the game in full-screen mode, without the ability to quickly switch between applications. The Windowed Full Screen option allows you to experience the game within a full-screen window, but be able to switch between applications by pressing the ATL+TAB keys on a PC.

**Display Resolution—**Based on which Window Mode you select, you can choose the resolution that the game will be displayed in. The options displayed will be based on the technical specifications of the computer you're using. By choosing Full Screen mode, you can view the game at a higher resolution.

**Frame Rate Limit—**The selected frame rate impacts the quality of the animation you'll see on the screen during the game. *Fortnite: Battle Royal* is a high-action game, where seeing as much detail as possible is equally important to being able to view smooth animations with no flickers or glitches. Ideally, you want to select at least 60 FPS (frames per second) rate. If you're using a higher-end PC, select the Unlimited option or any frame rate between 60 FPS and 240 FPS that your computer can smoothly display.

**Quality—**For this option, click on the Low, Medium, High, Epic, or Auto option. Start by selecting the Auto option. If you're not happy with the overall quality of the graphics and animations you're seeing during game play, experiment with the other options, starting from Epic and working your way down to Low. The Quality option refers to all graphics and animation displayed during game play. You can make further customizations by adjusting the next six options.

When adjusting any of the following options, only change one setting at a time by one increment. For example, if you change View Distance from Epic to Far, don't change anything else until you've tried playing a match and see firsthand how the graphics and animation look on your computer.

**3D Resolution**—This option allows you to manually select the resolution the graphics and animations are displayed using. Options start as low as 640 x 320 and go to 1366 x 768 (or beyond) depending on the capabilities of your monitor and graphics card. When you manually select between Low, Medium, High, Epic, or Auto for the Quality option, the 3D Resolution option will adjust accordingly, although you can override it.

**View Distance**—*Fortnite: Battle Royale* takes place on a massive island that you can freely explore during each match. The farther you can see off in the distance (what's ahead of you, to the sides, and behind you, for example), the better off you'll be. However, if you're using a lower-end computer you may need to lower the View Distance so nearby objects can be rendered faster and more clearly. If you're using a high-end computer, choose the Epic option. However, if you're using a computer with a slower processor or lower-end graphics card, you may need to select the Far, Medium, or Near option. Choosing the best option will likely involve some experimentation on your part. Start by choosing the Epic option, and work your way down, as needed, from Far to Medium and then Near.

**Shadows**—Being able to display shadows improves the overall look of the graphics and animations within the game, allowing you to see more detail. Better shadows also offer better depth perception, meaning objects will look more multi-dimensional. Accomplishing this requires a computer with a higher-end processor and graphics card. As with all of the other options offered below the Quality option, start by choosing Epic, and then work your way down from High to Medium to Off, as needed.

**Anti-Aliasing**—This is a programming technique that can improve graphic and animation quality, without adjusting resolution. Start by selecting the Epic option. If your computer can't handle it, work your way downward to High, Medium, and then Off.

**Textures**—When it comes to showcasing highly detailed graphics, textures allows you to see more detail when viewing otherwise flat objects. When textures is turned on and you're viewing the graphics and animation at a higher resolution, everything will look crisper, more vibrant, more multi-dimensional, and more detailed. However, lower-end computers might not be able to handle the processing power needed to display textures. Again, start by selecting the Epic option, and then work your way down, one step at a time to High, Medium, or Low, based on what your computer can handle. Based on the Quality and Resolution you've selected, the best Textures option will automatically be selected, but you can override it.

**Effects**—This is yet another option you can tweak to improve or decrease the quality of the graphics and animation you see when playing *Fortnite: Battle Royale* on your computer. It does not impact all graphics or animations, however. Go with the recommended setting for this option, unless you have a higher-end computer that'll support the Epic option.

**Post Processing**—Without impacting the quality of the graphics and animation too much, adjusting this setting could allow you to lower the Frame Rate Limit to reduce the amount of processing your computer and graphics card will need to do to display the best quality graphics and animation possible. Stick with the highest Frame Rate Limit your computer will support when playing *Fortnite: Battle Royale*, and adjust this option only if it becomes necessary to improve the graphics and animation quality. Most gamers are fine sticking with the setting recommended by their computer.

**Vsync—**This option applies when using Full Screen mode only. When turned on, it could improve the overall quality of the graphics and animations you see. The impact turning this feature on will have depends on the computer hardware you're using.

**Motion Blur—**The battle (firefight) sequences, and sometimes when gamers build, a lot of fast action is displayed on the screen. This can cause dizziness or nausea for some gamers, especially if you're sitting too close to your monitor. When turned on, you'll see more fluid and smooth animations. Turning this off will reduce the dizziness or nausea you may feel during the high-action events shown within the game.

**Show FPS—**Turning on this feature simply displays the current FPS that the computer is using to display the game's graphics and animation. While you're trying to figure out the best Display submenu settings to use, turn on this feature. However, once you've settled on settings that are working well on your computer, turn off this feature.

## ADJUSTING THE INPUT MENU OPTIONS

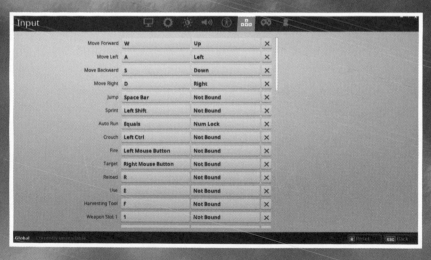

Every command, feature, and movement you make when playing *Fortnite: Battle Royale* is controlled by pressing a keyboard key or mouse button (unless you've connected a controller to your computer, in which case, refer to Section 4—Tweaking the Game Settings on a Console-Based System).

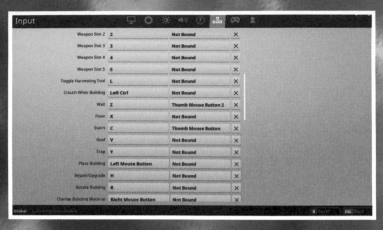

**Input**

| Weapon Slot 2 | 2 | Not Bound | ✕ |
| Weapon Slot 3 | 3 | Not Bound | ✕ |
| Weapon Slot 4 | 4 | Not Bound | ✕ |
| Weapon Slot 5 | 5 | Not Bound | ✕ |
| Toggle Harvesting Tool | L | Not Bound | ✕ |
| Crouch While Building | Left Ctrl | Not Bound | ✕ |
| Wall | Z | Thumb Mouse Button 2 | ✕ |
| Floor | X | Not Bound | ✕ |
| Stairs | C | Thumb Mouse Button | ✕ |
| Roof | V | Not Bound | ✕ |
| Trap | Y | Not Bound | ✕ |
| Place Building | Left Mouse Button | Not Bound | ✕ |
| Repair/Upgrade | H | Not Bound | ✕ |
| Rotate Building | R | Not Bound | ✕ |
| Change Building Material | Right Mouse Button | Not Bound | ✕ |

Global   Currently unavailable    R Reset   ESC Back

**Input**

| Select Building Edit | Left Mouse Button | Not Bound | ✕ |
| Reset Building Edit | Right Mouse Button | Not Bound | ✕ |
| Vehicle Exit | E | Not Bound | ✕ |
| Vehicle Change Seat | Left Ctrl | Not Bound | ✕ |
| Vehicle Honk Horn | Right Mouse Button | Not Bound | ✕ |
| ng Cart Push(Tap)/Coast(Hold) | Space Bar | Not Bound | ✕ |
| ATK Powerslide | Space Bar | Not Bound | ✕ |
| Trap Equip/Picker | F3 | Not Bound | ✕ |
| Previous Picker Wheel | Mouse Wheel Down | Not Bound | ✕ |
| Next Picker Wheel | Mouse Wheel Up | Not Bound | ✕ |
| Cursor Mode | Left Alt | Right Alt | ✕ |
| Switch Quickbar | Q | Not Bound | ✕ |
| Slot Up | Mouse Wheel Down | Not Bound | ✕ |
| Slot Down | Mouse Wheel Up | Not Bound | ✕ |
| Chat | Enter | Not Bound | ✕ |

These options allow you to change the primary and secondary key bindings for game actions.

Bindings for Vehicle Change Seat.

Global   Currently unavailable    R Reset   ESC Back

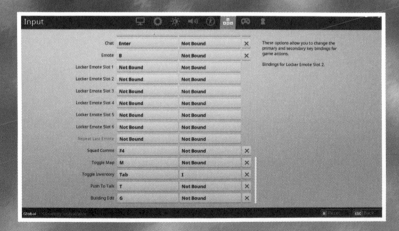

**Input**

| Chat | Enter | Not Bound | ✕ |
| Emote | B | Not Bound | ✕ |
| Locker Emote Slot 1 | Not Bound | Not Bound | |
| Locker Emote Slot 2 | Not Bound | Not Bound | |
| Locker Emote Slot 3 | Not Bound | Not Bound | |
| Locker Emote Slot 4 | Not Bound | Not Bound | |
| Locker Emote Slot 5 | Not Bound | Not Bound | |
| Locker Emote Slot 6 | Not Bound | Not Bound | |
| Repeat Last Emote | Not Bound | Not Bound | |
| Squad Comms | F4 | Not Bound | ✕ |
| Toggle Map | M | Not Bound | ✕ |
| Toggle Inventory | Tab | I | ✕ |
| Push To Talk | T | Not Bound | ✕ |
| Building Edit | G | Not Bound | ✕ |

These options allow you to change the primary and secondary key bindings for game actions.

Bindings for Locker Emote Slot 2.

Global   Currently unavailable    R Reset   ESC Back

Based on the keyboard you're using, the size of your hands, and your personal gaming style, you can leave the default options as is, or custom select a different keyboard key or mouse button for each command listed on this menu. To see the entire menu, you'll need to keep scrolling downward.

Whether you leave the keyboard and mouse commands at their default settings or opt to customize them, to become a top-notch *Fortnite: Battle Royale* player you'll need to memorize which keyboard key or mouse button is used for each option or command, and then be able to control the game without thinking too much about it. This will require you to, over time, train your muscle memory.

## WHAT IS KEY BINDING?

Anytime you reassign gaming tasks or functions to a different keyboard key or mouse button, this is referred to as key binding. If you choose to do this, one strategy is to assign specific *Fortnite: Battle Royale* game tasks you're already familiar with from similar games to the keys you're already accustomed to pressing in those games, since you've already trained your muscle memory. For example, consider binding the pickaxe to the "1" key, a rifle to the "2" key, a close-range weapon to the "3" key, and a sniper rifle (with a scope) to the "4" key.

Some top-ranked *Fortnite: Battle Royale* players have also changed the Ramp/Stair building key to the "E" key, for example, because it's easier to reach. Also, consider adding the Build Wall function to one of your side mouse buttons, again for convenience and because it's easier to reach. Doing this also makes it easier to place building tiles and start building, because this is all now done from the mouse.

Some gamers also find it more convenient to use the "C" key for crouching (by pressing it with your thumb), as opposed to using the default left CTRL key. Ultimately, bind keys with specific tasks so that they're comfortable and easily accessible to you—keeping in mind that your goal is to speed up how quickly you're able to execute commands and handle tasks within the game.

## WHAT IS MUSCLE MEMORY?

The concept of establishing and using your *muscle memory* applies when playing almost any computer or video game. The goal is to practice playing, and repeat the same actions so often that they become second nature to you. In other words, you train yourself to know exactly what to press on the keyboard and/or mouse, and know exactly when to do it, so you don't need to waste time thinking about it.

In terms of playing *Fortnite: Battle Royale*, with practice, you'll want to train your muscle memory to help you accomplish common tasks, including:

- Quickly switching between and selecting weapons within your backpack.
- Aiming your selected weapon and firing accurately at your targets.
- Switching between building, resource collection/harvesting, and fighting mode.
- Quickly building structures and being able to switch between building tile shapes and building materials.
- Accessing the island map, Emotes menu, and Quick Chat menu during a match.

## DO YOU REALLY NEED OPTIONAL EQUIPMENT?

If you take the time to watch the live streams of the top-ranked *Fortnite: Battle Royale* players, you'll see that almost all of them use a high-end PC that's equipped with an optional gaming keyboard, gaming mouse, and gaming headset. Adding this optional equipment to your computer can cost an extra $300.00 to $400.00 (or more), but could give you a speed and response time advantage when playing *Fortnite: Battle Royale*.

Another reason why gamers like to add this optional and specialized equipment to their setup is because it looks really awesome. Gaming keyboards, for example, often have LED-colored backlighting (lights below each key), so you can color-code them and play in a dark room.

Gaming keyboards also have mechanical keyswitches which react faster to repetitive key presses that relate to specific gaming commands, like firing a weapon. Some gaming keyboards also have built-in memory, so you can store custom game configurations. Many companies offer gaming keyboards that cost between $100.00 and $200.00. Several are listed within Section 6—*Fortnite: Battle Royale* Resources.

Shown here is the Corsair K70 RGB MK.2 keyboard ($169.99, www.corsair.com).

Many companies also offer optional gaming mice. Yes, they work very much like most other mice, but these are souped-up and designed to meet the precision and speed requirements of gamers. The Corsair Glaive RGB Gaming Mouse ($49.99, www.corsair .com) is shown here.

An optional gaming mouse, like the Corsair Glaive RGB Gaming Mouse, offers enhanced movement precision using 16,000 DPI optical sensor technology, as well as an ergonomic design so it remains comfortable under your hand during extended gaming sessions. This mouse also offers three interchangeable magnetic grips, so it'll adapt in seconds to provide a gamer with a customized fit. The mouse buttons are designed for ultra-fast click response and durability. They're rated for up to 50 million clicks.

Like gaming keyboards, some gaming mice also offer built-in LED color lights that are customizable, which is more for cosmetic purposes than functionality, but the LED lights look awesome.

If your computer already has a regular keyboard and mouse, and you don't want to spend the cash on an upgrade, one optional accessory that will definitely help you improve your game is a gaming headset with a built-in microphone.

Anytime you're playing *Fortnite: Battle Royale*'s Duos, Squads, or a 50 v 50 game, for example, you'll definitely want to talk to your partner, squad mates, or team members, while hearing all of the game's sound effects. Even if you're playing the Solo game play mode, you'll definitely want to use stereo headphones or a gaming headset that'll allow you to clearly hear the game's sound effects.

Shown here is one of Turtle Beach Corp.'s corded gaming headsets. The company has a selection of corded and wireless (Bluetooth) headsets compatible with all computers and gaming systems. They range in price from $59.95 to $299.95. For more information, visit: www.turtlebeach.com.

## IMPROVE YOUR INTERNET CONNECTION

To have the greatest success playing *Fortnite: Battle Royale* will require a fast and reliable continuous Internet connection. To speed up your Internet connection and help ensure it remains stable during game play, instead of relying on a Wi-Fi Internet connection, plug your computer directly into your home's Internet modem or router using an Ethernet cable. If your computer does not have a built-in Ethernet port, consider buying a USB Ethernet adapter.

Within the Search field of Amazon.com or any Internet search engine, type "USB Ethernet adapter" to find a compatible adapter for your Windows or MacOS-based computer system. Choose an adapter that supports USB 3.0 and 10/100/1000 Mbps Ethernet speeds. The cost of the adapter should be less than $25.00.

If you're using an Apple MacBook Air, for example, that does not have a built-in Ethernet port, use the Apple USB Ethernet Adapter ($29.00, www.apple.com/shop/product/MC704LL/A/apple-usb-ethernet-adapter) or the Apple Thunderbolt to Gigabit Ethernet Adapter ($29.00, www.apple.com/shop/product/MD463LL/A/thunderbolt-to-gigabit-ethernet-adapter).

# SECTION 4

## TWEAKING THE GAME SETTINGS ON A CONSOLE-BASED SYSTEM

If you're a PlayStation 4, Xbox One, or Nintendo Switch gamer, while accessing *Fortnite: Battle Royale*'s Settings menus in order to personalize your game play experience, you'll definitely want to choose a controller layout that best fits your gaming style. The default option is called Old School, and it's great for noobs.

However, if your primary focus while playing *Fortnite: Battle Royale* is more on building, you'll want to choose between the Quick Builder or Builder Pro controller layouts. Gamers who focus more on combat during matches will want to select the Combat Pro controller layout. Ultimately, which you choose is a matter of personal preference.

Whichever controller layout you go with, memorize the buttons and practice being able to fight, explore, and build during a match very quickly. For example, being able to switch between weapons, target a weapon, and accurately fire on your enemies will take practice, but the first step is knowing exactly which controller buttons to press and when.

## THE OLD SCHOOL CONTROLLER LAYOUT

Here's the Old School controller layout on each of the console-based gaming systems. Unlike when playing the PC or Mac version, you cannot customize each controller button, but you can choose between four different controller layouts.

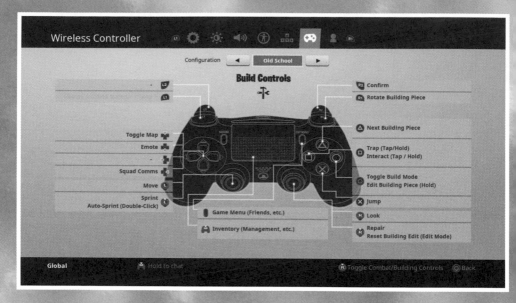

PlayStation 4

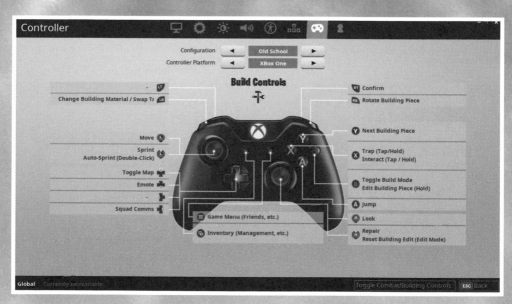

Xbox One

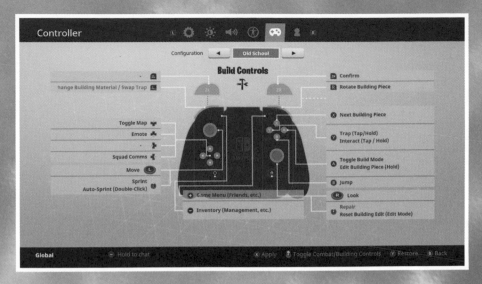

Nintendo Switch

# THE QUICK BUILDER CONTROLLER LAYOUT

Each of the controller layouts repositions key actions or movements your soldier will need to take during a match, making them easier to access based on your personal gaming style and your primary strategy focus.

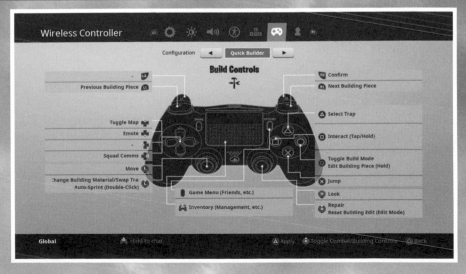

PlayStation 4

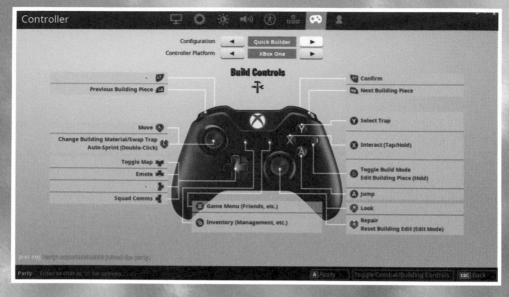

Xbox One

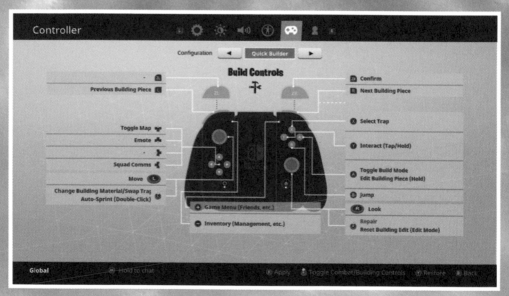

Nintendo Switch

## HE BUILDER PRO CONTROLLER LAYOUT

In the early days of *Fortnite: Battle Royale*, building played a major role in a gamer's success. Building was particularly important during the End Game. Since Epic Games has tweaked the game over the past few months, building elaborate fortresses and structures is less critical. However, you'll definitely still need to build ramps, bridges, and smaller structures throughout matches. Thus, developing and practicing your building skills is still important.

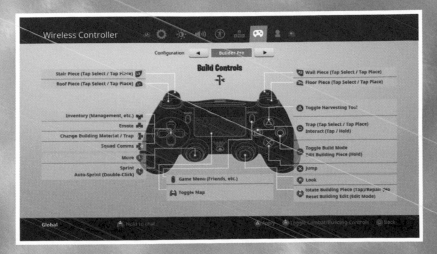

PlayStation 4

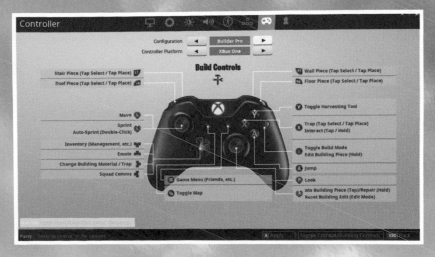

Xbox One

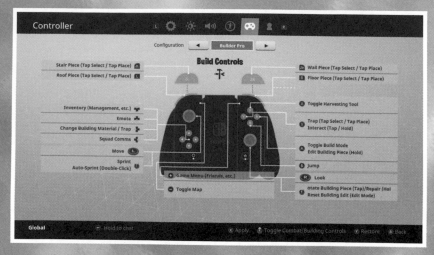

Nintendo Switch

## THE COMBAT PRO CONTROLLER LAYOUT

*Fortnite: Battle Royale* continues to be an action-intensive combat adventure game. Being able to engage in firefights and battles, react quickly, and expertly utilize the weapons at your disposal is absolutely essential. Once you start improving your gaming skills when it comes to surviving during matches, consider using the Combat Pro controller layout, which makes all of the commands and game-related features needed for combat readily accessible.

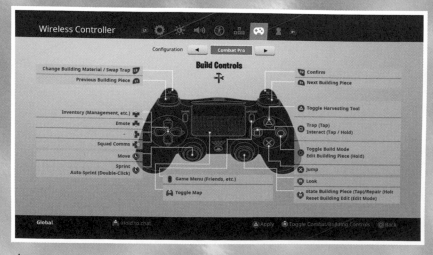

PlayStation 4

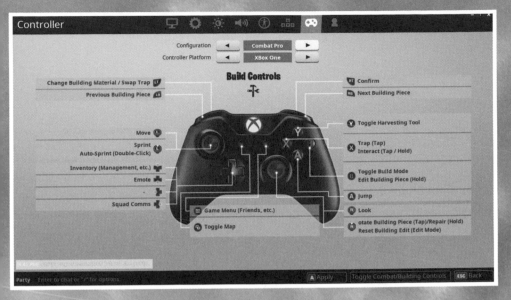

Xbox One

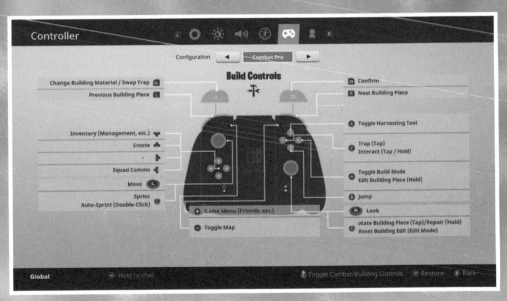

Nintendo Switch

## SHOULD YOU USE AN OPTIONAL CONTROLLER?

The PlayStation 4 comes with the Sony DualShock 4 Wireless Controller, while the Xbox One comes with the Microsoft Xbox Wireless Controller. Both are well-suited for playing *Fortnite: Battle Royale*.

For Xbox gamers, Microsoft offers the online-based Xbox Design Lab (https://xboxdesignlab.xbox.com). For $69.99, you can custom design the color scheme of your own Xbox One Wireless Controller. These controllers offer the same layout and performance as the regular Xbox Wireless Controller, but you can choose the controller's appearance by selecting the color of the controller's body, back, bumpers, triggers, D-Pad, thumbsticks, and ABXY buttons.

The Nintendo Switch's built-in controller is *not* so ideal for *Fortnite: Battle Royale*, but it does work when you're playing on the go. If you get serious about improving your gaming skills and timing, especially when it comes to building and combat, definitely invest in the optional Nintendo Switch Pro Controller ($69.99).

There are many optional controllers available from companies besides Sony, Microsoft, and Nintendo that offer optional controller alternatives for the console-based systems. For example, there's a company called Razer (www.razer.com/console) that offers the slick Razer Wolverine Tournament Edition controller for the Xbox One ($119.99).

For the PS4, a company called SCUFGaming (www.scufgaming.com/vantage) offers the Vantage wireless controller ($199.95). A wired edition is available for $169.95. These can be purchased wherever gaming systems are sold. However, from the company's website, you're able to customize the color scheme of the controller's faceplate, rings, thumbsticks, control disc, and trigger system. (Visit: https://scufgaming.com/scuf-vantage-custom-ps4-controller).

When choosing an optional controller for your PS4, Xbox One, or Nintendo Switch, choose one that's equal or better quality than the controller that came with your gaming system, and that offers some type of competitive advantage, such as a better grip, smoother buttons, or faster response time. Beware of low-end optional controllers from companies you've never heard of. These often cost less money, but they offer poor quality that can actually be detrimental to your experience and success rate when playing *Fortnite: Battle Royale*.

## IMPROVE YOUR INTERNET CONNECTION

Having a reliable and fast continuous Internet connection is also essential when playing *Fortnite: Battle Royale*. Instead of relying on your console system's Wi-Fi (wireless) connection to your in-home Internet, you'll often achieve faster Internet speed if you connect your gaming system directly to your modem or router using an optional Ethernet cable.

The PlayStation 4 and Xbox One have a built-in Ethernet port, so you simply need to connect a compatible Ethernet cable from the back of your gaming console to your Internet modem or router.

For the Nintendo Switch, Nintendo offers the Wii LAN Adapter ($24.99), but there's also the Hori Wired Internet LAN Adapter ($29.99, http://stores.horiusa.com/lan-adapter-for-nintendo-switch). Either connects to one of the USB ports on the Nintendo Switch's dock and allows you to connect an Ethernet cable between the gaming system and your Internet modem or router.

For more information about how to use this accessory, visit: https://en-americas-support.nintendo.com/app/answers/detail/a_id/22544/~/how-to-install-a-lan-adapter-to-nintendo-switch.

# SECTION 5

## PERSONALIZING YOUR *FORTNITE: BATTLE ROYALE* EXPERIENCE ON A MOBILE DEVICE

**E**pic Games has done an amazing job adapting the full version of *Fortnite: Battle Royale* to the Apple iPhone smartphone, Apple iPad tablet, and many Android-based smartphones and tablets. The screenshots within this section were captured using an iPad Pro or iPhone X.

To improve your gaming experience when playing the mobile version, from the Lobby you're able to customize a wide range of options from the Settings menu, but also take full advantage of the exclusive HUB Layout Tool. To access these options, from the Lobby (shown here on an iPad), tap on the Menu icon that's displayed in the top-right corner of the screen. It looks like three horizontal lines.

Shown here is the Lobby screen on an iPhone. As you can see, it displays virtually identical content to all other versions of *Fortnite: Battle Royale*.

Displayed in the top-right corner of the screen is the game's main menu. Tap on the Controls Help button to see the on-screen controller icons (the HUD display) and how they're used when playing *Fortnite: Battle Royale*.

## MEMORIZE THE HUD LAYOUT

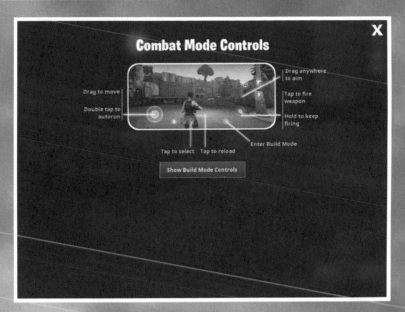

Shown here is the Combat Mode Controls layout, which you can customize using the HUD Layout Tool.

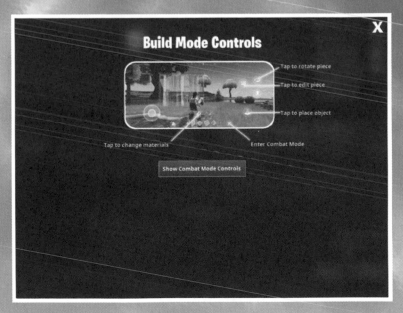

Shown here is the Build Mode Controls layout, which can also be customized using the HUD Layout Tool.

Whether you use the default settings shown here, or you use the HUD Layout Tool to customize the appearance of the game screen, you definitely need to memorize the layout, so you can react quickly when fighting and building, for example, by knowing exactly where and when to tap on the screen to achieve the results you need.

## THE SETTINGS SUBMENUS

From the game's main menu, tap on the gear-shaped Settings option to access the Settings submenus. Displayed along the top of the screen are four command icons to access each submenu. There's the Video (shown here on an iPhone), Game, Audio, and Account submenus.

From the Video menu, you can select the overall quality of the graphics and animation you'll see on the screen. For most mobile devices, select the Epic option to experience the best possible graphics.

However, if your mobile device is older, or having trouble displaying the graphics and animations in Epic mode, choose the Auto mode, and let the game adjust this setting for you.

When you tap on the Mobile Framerate option, you can switch between 20 and 30 FPS (frames per second). Once again, choose the highest listed option first. Only choose a lower option if your smartphone or tablet is having trouble displaying the game's graphics and animation.

If you turn on the Allow Low Power Mode, the game will automatically turn off certain less essential in-game features in order to preserve power so you can play longer without recharging your mobile device. For the best gaming experience possible, turn off this feature. However, if you need your smartphone or tablet's battery to last a bit longer, turn on this feature.

The customizable options offered under the Game submenu (shown here) are virtually identical to the options offered by this menu when playing any other version of *Fortnite: Battle Royale*. Refer back to Section 2—Discover What You Can Do from the Game Submenu.

One option offered in the Game submenu within the mobile version of the game is called Motion Enabled (see page 87). This can be turned on or off. When turned on, you can adjust your view of the game screen by moving the mobile device itself. For example, if you want your soldier to look up, you'd tilt your smartphone or tablet slightly upward. Some gamers like this feature, others don't, so whether or not you turn it on is a matter of personal preference.

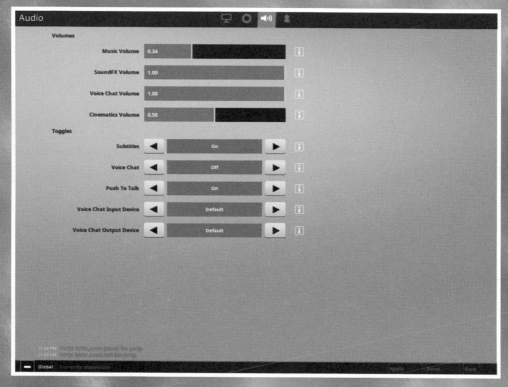

The Audio menu offers all the customizable options already described within Section 1—Overview of *Fortnite: Battle Royale*. Instead of connecting an optional gaming headset to your smartphone or tablet (which is recommended), you can turn on the Voice Chat feature, as well as the Push to Talk option, and then use your mobile device's built-in speaker and microphone to speak with your partner, squad mates, or team members when playing a Duos, Squads, or 50 v 50 match, for example.

If you want to use stereo headphones with a built-in microphone, such as Apple's AirPods or Apple's EarPods with your iPhone or iPad, pair or connect this accessory to your smartphone or tablet, and then adjust the options for Voice Chat Input Device and Voice Chat Output Device. Select the iOS-Audio-Unit-Capture and iOS-Audio-Unit-Render options respectively. Android-based mobile device users should select the similar options that are offered.

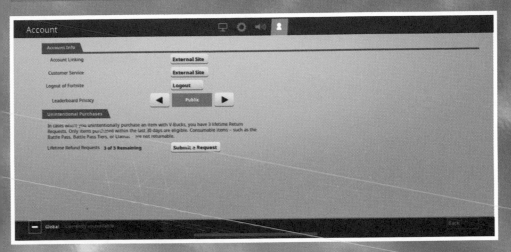

The options found within the Account submenu (shown here on an iPhone) are identical to what you'd find in other versions of the game. You'll typically just want to leave these options at their default settings.

## HOW TO USE THE HUD LAYOUT TOOL

The HUD Layout Tool allows you to customize the "heads up display," which are the on-screen controls you'll use throughout the game to control your soldier.

To customize the HUD display, before a match, from the Lobby, access the game's main menu (shown here on an iPhone). This time tap on the HUD Layout Tool button that's displayed near the top-right corner of the screen.

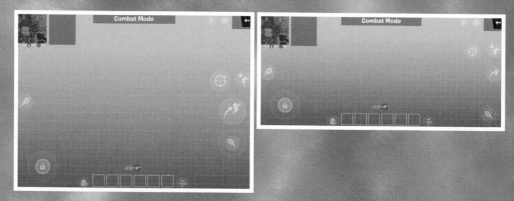

Starting with the Combat Mode screen, you're able to move around or resize almost every on-screen icon that's displayed in white. You can also move around the Location Map (mini-map) that by default is displayed in the top-left corner of the screen.

This is the same screen, shown on an iPhone.

The changes you make to either the Combat Mode or Build Mode HUD layout should be based on two important criteria. First, consider how you hold your smartphone or tablet in your hands when playing *Fortnite: Battle Royale*. You'll want all of the important icons to be easily accessible using your thumbs or fingers, based on how you'll be holding the mobile device.

Second, consider your gaming style and how you'd prefer to organize the icons on the game screen. You might want to experience several matches using the default settings for both the Combat Mode and Build Mode screens, and then make adjustments based on your personal gaming style and preferences.

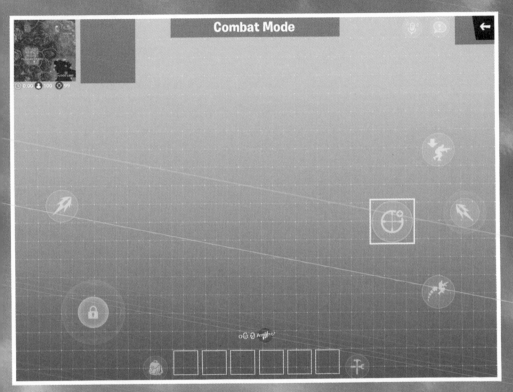

When you're viewing the HUD Layout Tool for either Combat Mode or Build Mode, place your finger on any of the white icons and drag it to the desired location. You can't move the boxes displayed in grey (that during game play display information), but you can move the Location Map.

# HOW TO RESIZE ON-SCREEN ICONS

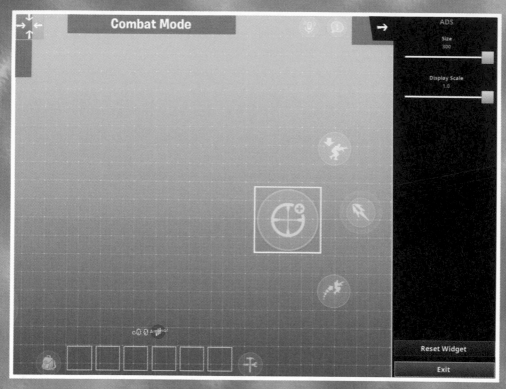

To resize any of the white icons, first tap on the icon you want to change to highlight it. A yellow border will appear around it. Next, tap on the left-pointing arrow icon that's displayed in the top-right corner of the screen. Within the right column, you'll see two sliders—Size and Display Scale. Move the Size slider to the right to make the on-screen icon larger, or to the left to make it smaller. Press the right-pointing arrow at the top of this menu to return to the main HUD Layout Tool screen and select a different icon to resize. Keep in mind, after resizing an icon, you may need to reposition it on the screen.

> If you're playing on an iPhone X (or later) model, when holding the phone in landscape mode (horizontally), you'll need to move several of the icons that are displayed along the right-edge of the screen over a bit to the left to make them more easily visible and accessible while playing.

# HOW TO SWITCH BETWEEN CONTROL MODES AND ADJUST THE FIRE MODE OPTION

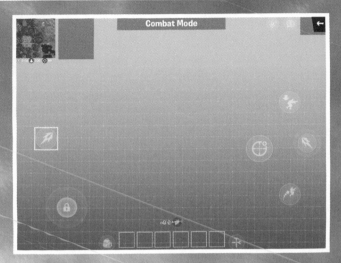

Without first highlighting and selecting one of the on-screen icons, when you're looking at the HUD Layout Tool for either Combat Mode or Build Mode, tap on the left-pointing arrow icon that's displayed in the top-right corner of the screen.

From the menu that's displayed, switch between the Combat Mode screen and the Build Mode screen by tapping on either option. Tap on the Change Fire Mode option to switch between the three ways to fire a weapon. This is a unique feature available only in the mobile version of *Fortnite: Battle Royale*.

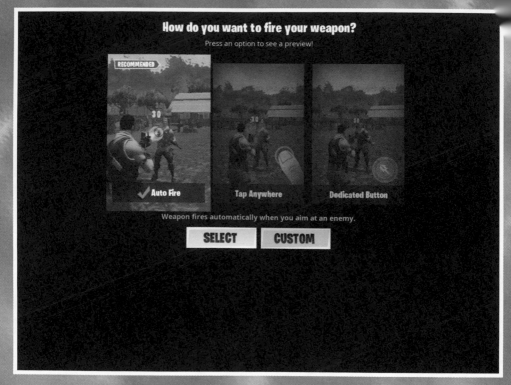

After tapping on the Change Fire Mode option, choose between Auto Fire, Tap Anywhere, and Dedicated Button to determine how you'll fire the weapon your soldier is holding during a match. To make your decision, tap on one of the three options displayed, or tap on the Custom button.

The Auto Fire option will automatically fire the selected weapon for you when you aim it at an enemy soldier. (If you aim at a structure, building, or object, you'll still need to aim and then manually fire the selected weapon.) For most gamers, this is the preferred setting.

The Tap Anywhere option allows you to fire the selected weapon by tapping anywhere on the game screen (using either thumb or any finger).

By selecting the Dedicated Button, you'll only be able to fire the selected weapon when you press the Trigger button after aiming your soldier's weapon.

By tapping on the Custom button, from the "How Do You Want to Fire Your Weapon?" menu, select one, two, or all three options. Make your selection(s) and tap on the Select button.

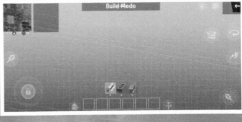

On the left is what the default HUD layout for Build Mode looks like. Once again, you can resize and/or reposition any of the icons displayed in white, along with the Location Map.

On the right is the same screen shown on an iPhone.

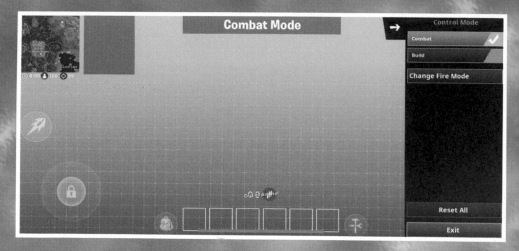

When you return to the Control Mode menu (shown here on an iPhone), you can now switch to the Build Mode HUD Layout Tool, tap on the Reset All button to reset all of the options to their default settings, or tap on the Exit button to save your changes.

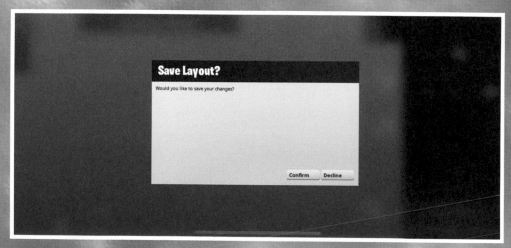

Be sure to tap on the Confirm button to save your changes when this Save Layout? pop-up window appears (shown on an iPhone). All of the changes you've made to the HUD layout will remain active until you return to the HUD Layout Tool and manually make changes or tap on the Reset All button. Upon tapping the Confirm button, you'll be returned to the game's main menu. Tap anywhere in the bottom-half of the screen to return to the Lobby.

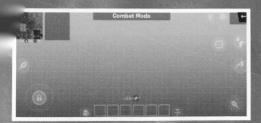

When you're viewing either the Combat Mode (shown here on an iPhone) or Build Mode HUD Layout Tool screens, place your finger near the top of the screen and drag it downward slightly. The Extra Buttons menu is displayed. You can now drag any of these buttons down onto the main HUD layout. The numbered icons each refer to a Resource or Backpack Inventory Slot.

You're now ready to choose a game play mode, and then tap on the Play option to enter into a match.

# OPTIONAL CONTROLLERS ARE AVAILABLE FOR MOBILE DEVICES

If you want to make your gaming experience even more like playing *Fortnite: Battle Royale* on a computer or console-based system, add an optional controller to your mobile device. To find optional game controllers compatible with the iPhone, iPad, or your Android-based gaming system, within the Search field of your favorite Internet search engine, type "iPhone Game Controller," "iPad Game Controller," or "Android Game Controller."

There's the SteelSeries Stratus Wireless Gaming Controller for iPhone, iPad, and iPod Touch ($35.00) or the SteelSeries Nimbus Wireless Controller ($49.95). A similar version of these controllers is available for Android-based mobile devices. For more information, visit: www.steelseries.com/gaming-controllers.

For smartphones, the GameSir T1 Wireless Bluetooth Game Controller ($29.99, www.gamesir.hk/collections/gamepads) clips onto and holds your iPhone or Android-based smartphone while giving you access to a full-size gaming controller that's similar to the PS4, Xbox One, or Nintendo Switch Pro Controller.

The GameVice Controller Gamepad ($99.95, www.gamevice.com) is a two-piece controller that clips onto either end of your smartphone or tablet. Several versions are available, so choose the correct one for your smartphone or tablet model.

# SECTION 6

## FORTNITE: BATTLE ROYALE RESOURCES

On YouTube (www.youtube.com) or Twitch.TV (www.twitch.tv /directory/game/Fortnite), in the Search field, enter the search phrase "*Fortnite: Battle Royale*" to discover many game-related channels, live streams, and prerecorded videos that'll help you become a better player.

## OPTIONAL GAMING ACCESSORY COMPANIES

Here's a listing of companies that offer optional gaming accessories, including: gaming keyboards and gaming mice for PCs and Macs, gaming headsets, and gaming controllers.

- Corsair—www.corsair.com
- GameSir—www.gamesir.hk/collections/gamepads
- GameVice—www.gamevice.com
- HyperX—www.hyperxgaming.com
- Razer—www.razer.com
- Roccat—www.roccat.org
- SCUFGaming—www.scufgaming.com/vantage
- SteelSeries—www.steelseries.com/gaming-controllers
- Turtle Beach Corp.—www.turtlebeach.com
- Xbox Design Lab—https://xboxdesignlab.xbox.com

## *FORTNITE: BATTLE ROYALE* ONLINE RESOURCES

Also, be sure to check out these online resources related to *Fortnite: Battle Royale*:

| WEBSITE OR YOUTUBE CHANNEL NAME | DESCRIPTION | URL |
| --- | --- | --- |
| Best *Fortnite* Settings | Discover the custom game settings used by some of the world's top-rated *Fortnite: Battle Royale* players. | www.bestfortnitesettings. com |
| Fandom's *Fortnite* Wiki | Discover the latest news and strategies related to *Fortnite: Battle Royale*. | http://fortnite.wikia.com/ wiki/Fortnite_Wiki |
| FantasticalGamer | A popular YouTuber who publishes *Fortnite* tutorial videos. | www.youtube.com/user/ FantasticalGamer |
| FBR Insider | The *Fortnite: Battle Royale Insider* website offers game-related news, tips, and strategy videos. | www.fortniteinsider.com |
| *Fortnite* Config | An independent website that lists the custom game settings for dozens of top-rated *Fortnite: Battle Royale* players. | https://fortniteconfig.com |
| *Fortnite* Gamepedia Wiki | Read up-to-date descriptions of every weapon, loot item, and ammo type available within *Fortnite: Battle Royale*. This Wiki also maintains a comprehensive database of soldier outfits and related items released by Epic Games. | https://fortnite.gamepedia. com/Fortnite_Wiki |
| *Fortnite Intel* | An independent source of news related to *Fortnite: Battle Royale*. | www.fortniteintel.com |

| | | |
|---|---|---|
| *Fortnite* Scout | Check your personal player stats, and analyze your performance using a bunch of colorful graphs and charts. Also check out the stats of other *Fortnite: Battle Royale* players. | www.fortnitescout.com |
| *Fortnite* Stats & Leaderboard | This is an independent website that allows you to view your own *Fortnite*-related stats or discover the stats from the best players in the world. | https://fortnitestats.com |
| *Game Informer* Magazine's *Fortnite* Coverage | Discover articles, reviews, and news about *Fortnite: Battle Royale* published by *Game Informer* magazine. | www.gameinformer.com/search/searchresults.aspx?q=Fortnite |
| *Game Skinny* Online Guides | A collection of topic-specific strategy guides related to *Fortnite*. | www.gameskinny.com/tag/fortnite-guides/ |
| GameSpot's *Fortnite* Coverage | Check out the news, reviews, and game coverage related to *Fortnite: Battle Royale* that's been published by GameSpot. | www.gamespot.com/fortnite |
| IGN Entertainment's *Fortnite* Coverage | Check out all IGN's past and current coverage of *Fortnite*. | www.ign.com/wikis/fortnite |
| Jason R. Rich's Website and Social Media Feeds | Share your *Fortnite: Battle Royale* game play strategies with this book's author and learn about his other books. | www.JasonRich.com www.FortniteGameBooks.com Twitter: @JasonRich7 Instagram: @JasonRich7 |
| Microsoft's Xbox One *Fortnite* Website | Learn about and acquire *Fortnite: Battle Royale* if you're an Xbox One gamer. | www.microsoft.com/en-US/store/p/Fortnite-Battle-Royalee/BT5P2X999VH2 |
| MonsterDface YouTube and Twitch.tv Channels | Watch video tutorials and live game streams from an expert *Fortnite* player. | www.youtube.com/user/MonsterdfaceLive www.Twitch.tv/MonsterDface |

*(continued on next pag*

| Ninja | Check out the live and recorded game streams from Ninja, one of the most highly skilled *Fortnite: Battle Royale* players in the world on Twitch.tv and YouTube. | www.twitch.tv/ ninja_fortnite_hyper www.youtube.com/user/ NinjasHyper |
|---|---|---|
| Official Epic Games YouTube Channel for *Fortnite: Battle Royale* | The official *Fortnite: Battle Royale* YouTube channel. | www.youtube.com/user/ epicfortnite |
| ProSettings.com | An independent website that lists the custom game settings for top-ranked *Fortnite: Battle Royale* players. This website also recommends optional gaming accessories, such as keyboards, mice, graphics cards, controllers, gaming headsets, and monitors. | www.prosettings.com/ game/fortnite www.prosettings.com/ best-fortnite-settings |
| Turtle Beach Corp. | This is one of many companies that make great-quality, wired or wireless (Bluetooth) gaming headsets that work with all gaming platforms. | www.turtlebeach.com |

## YOUR *FORTNITE: BATTLE ROYALE* ADVENTURE CONTINUES . . .

One important lesson that you've hopefully learned from this unofficial strategy guide is that when it comes to playing *Fortnite: Battle Royale*, if you have dreams and aspirations to become one of the world's top-ranked players, milliseconds matter!

Through countless hours of practice, you need to hone your gaming skills so that you're able to make decisions quickly, and then react and take action within the game even faster. Whether you're building, participating in a firefight, trying to evade an enemy, driving an All Terrain Vehicle, exploring, or simply attempting to survive until the very last moments of an End Game, speed and reaction times matter!

Just as your own reflexes and thought processes need to be fast, so does the technology you're using. Your continuous Internet connection should be as fast and reliable as possible, and if your gaming system is a computer, you want to take advantage of a fast processor, powerful graphics card, as well as a mouse and keyboard that are designed for gaming, so that you don't experience any lagging during a match.

Meanwhile, if you're experiencing *Fortnite: Battle Royale* on a console-based system, you definitely want to utilize the highest-quality, most precise, and fastest-reacting controller you can get your hands on.

And finally, to potentially shave milliseconds off of your in-game actions, it's important to tweak the options available from the *Fortnite: Battle Royale* Settings menus, so each of the options is customized based on your skill level, gaming style, personal preferences, and the equipment you're using.

Once all of your technology is set up correctly, start to focus on your actual gaming skills and putting in the countless hours of practice that'll be needed to win matches, achieve #1 Victory Royale, and eventually have your username displayed on the official *Fortnite: Battle Royale* leaderboards.

This unofficial guide has helped you to fine-tune your in-game settings and personalize your overall game play experience. You'll now want to read additional strategy guides that focus on specific tips and strategies related to exploration, building, survival, combat, and actually playing *Fortnite: Battle Royale*.

Oh, and one final piece of advice . . . don't forget to have fun playing, and good luck!